PROLETERKA

PROLETERKA

Fleur Jaeggy

Translated by Alastair McEwen

SHEFFIELD – LONDON – NEW YORK

This edition is the first UK publication. It was published in 2019 by
And Other Stories
Sheffield – London – New York
www.andotherstories.org

First published as *Proleterka* in 2001 by Adelphi Edizioni S.P.A, Milan
© 2001 Adelphi Edizioni S.P.A., Milan
English-language translation © 2003 by Alastair McEwen
This translation first published in 2003 in the USA by New Directions, with
the title *SS Proleterka*.

9 8 7 6 5 4 3 2 1

ISBN: 978-1911508-56-4
eBook ISBN: 978-1911508-57-1

Proofreader: Sarah Terry; Typesetter: Tetragon, London; Typefaces: Linotype
Swift Neue and Verlag; Cover Design: Edward Bettison. Printed and bound by
the CPI Group (UK) Ltd, Croydon, CRO 4YY.

A catalogue record for this book is available from the British Library.

This book was supported using public funding by Arts Council England.

Many years have gone by and this morning I have a sudden desire: I would like my father's ashes. After the cremation, they sent me a small object that had resisted the fire. A nail. They returned it intact. I wondered then if they had really left it in his suit pocket. It must burn with Johannes, I had told the staff of the crematorium. They were not to take it out of his pocket. In his hands it would have been too visible. Today I would like his ashes. It will probably be an urn like any other. The name engraved on a plate. A bit like a soldier's dog tags. Why was it then that it had not occurred to me to ask for the ashes?

At that time I didn't use to think about the dead. They come to us late. They call when they sense that we have become prey and it is time for the hunt. When Johannes died I didn't think he really died.

I took part in the funeral. Nothing else. After the service, I left right away. It was an azure day, everything was done. Miss Gerda saw to all the details. For this I am grateful to her. She made an appointment with the hairdresser for me. She got me a black suit. Discreet. She scrupulously complied with Johannes's wishes.

I saw my father for the last time in a cold place. I bade him farewell. Miss Gerda was at my side. I was dependent on her for everything. I did not know what one does when a person dies. She had a precise knowledge of all the formalities. She is efficient, silent, timidly sorrowful. Like an ax, she advances through the meanderings of grief. When it comes to making choices, she has no doubts. She was so thorough. I was unable to be even a little bit sad. She took all the sadness. But I would have given her the sadness in any case. There was nothing left for me.

I tell her that I would like to be alone for a moment. A few minutes. The cold room was freezing. In those few minutes I put the nail in the pocket of Johannes's gray suit. I did not want to look at him. His face is in my mind, in my eyes. I have no need to look at him. But I did the opposite. I looked at him rather well, to see, and to know, if there were signs of suffering. And this was a mistake. For, in looking at him so attentively, his face eluded me. I forgot his physiognomy, his real face, the usual one.

Miss Gerda has come to fetch me. I try to kiss Johannes on the brow. She recoils in sudden revulsion and stops me. It had been such a sudden desire this morning, to want Johannes's ashes. Now it has vanished.

I did not know my father very well. One Easter holiday he took me with him on a cruise. The ship was moored in Venice. Her name was *Proleterka. The Proletarian Lass.* For years the occasion of our meetings had been a procession. We both took part. We paraded together through the streets of a city on a lake. He with his tricorne on his head. I in the *Tracht*, the traditional costume with the black bonnet trimmed in white lace. The black patent-leather shoes with the grosgrain buckles. The silk apron over the red of the costume, a red beneath which a dark bluish-purple lurked. And the bodice in damasked silk. In a square, atop a pyre of wood, they were burning an effigy. The *Böögg*. Men on horseback gallop in a circle around the fire. Drums roll. Standards are raised. They were bidding the winter farewell. To me it seemed like bidding farewell to something I had never had. I was drawn to the flames. It was a long time ago.

My father, Johannes H., was a member of a Guild, a *Zunft*. He joined it when he was a student. He had written a report called *What the Guild Did and What It Could Have Done During the War.* The Guild to which Johannes belonged was founded in 1336.

On the previous evening there had been the children's ball. A big hall thronged with costumes and laughter. I was

9

waiting for it all to be over. Perhaps Johannes was too. I do not like balls, and I wanted to take my costume off. The first time I took part in the procession (I had not yet started school) they put me in a sky-blue sedan chair. From the window, I waved at the other children who were watching the procession from the pavement. When the porters set me down on the ground, I opened the door and went off. I had not thought to run away. It was not rebellion, but pure instinct. A desire for the unknown. For hours I wandered through the city. Until I was exhausted. The police found me. And they handed me over to my lawful owner, Johannes. I was sorry. Given the circumstances, any chance of a more profound acquaintance between father and daughter was limited in the extreme. Observe and keep quiet. The two walk close to each other in the procession. They do not exchange a word. The father has trouble keeping in step with the march music. Two shadows, one moving slowly, with a visible effort. The other more restless. The people proceed in ranks of four. Beside them, a couple; the man in military uniform, the woman in costume. They are in step, their gait majestic, sanctified, proud. Heads held high. At night, sometimes, the burning effigy would return beneath closed eyelids. The roll of the drums even more martial, with a posthumous sound. In a hotel room, two days later, I left Johannes. The term of my visit had expired.

Proleterka had been chartered by some gentlemen who belonged to the same Guild as Johannes. The ones who paraded through the city in the month of April. They were to be our traveling companions. We set off, my father and I, by train for Venice. The carriage was empty. From that moment I would be with Johannes, my father. He is not yet seventy years old. White hair, parted, straight. Pale, gelid eyes. Unnatural. Like a fairy tale about ice. Wintry eyes. With a glimmer of romantic caprice. The irises of such a clear, faded green that they made you feel uneasy. It is almost as if they lack the consistency of a gaze. As if it were an anomaly, generations old. Johannes had a twin brother, with similar eyes. His brother's eyes were often concealed by his eyelids. He would spend hours in the garden. In a wheelchair. He could manage to say: "*Es ist kalt,*" it's cold. His tone held a blend of the awareness of a divine imposition and the mere earthly realization that cold is transitory. As was his illness. In those days they called it sleeping sickness.

In the compartment, Johannes is reading the newspaper. He reads for a long time. Perhaps he does not know what to say to me. I observe the fingers that hold the newspaper, and his shoes. I cast about for a topic of conversation. I do not find one. I think of the word *Proleterka*, the name of the Yugoslavian ship. There are more beautiful names for ships. Like the *Indomitable*, on which Billy Budd was hanged. Do you remember when the chaplain visits the sailor in irons in order to sow the idea of death in him? Billy Budd's last words were: "God bless Captain Vere!" He blesses the man who ordered his execution. He blessed his executioner. I should like to talk to you of Billy Budd, instead of telling this brief story hoisted from the yard-arm, swaying before a headwind at the mercy of nothingness. Billy Budd, I see him as the landscape slips by, while the hours slip by in the company of Johannes. We do not know who Billy Budd's father was, or where he was born. They found him in a

11

pretty little basket lined with silk. I know Billy Budd much better than I know my father. "We're here," says Johannes. We have no luggage. It is on the ship. The *Proleterka*.

Father and daughter take the vaporetto to Piazza San Marco. The daughter looks farther and farther ahead; she wants to see the ship. Venice appears and disappears. They walk along the Riva degli Schiavoni. The daughter is impatient. Johannes walks slowly. He has a malformation of the foot. He wears shoes that are a bit high at the ankles.

I used to think that he was born that way. And that he had always had difficulty walking. But it had been caused by a carcinoma. I read this in an album, the traditional kind they give when a child is born. It records the first days of life, the first months, almost day by day. On the eighteenth month, Johannes notes that his daughter had gone to visit him in hospital. If she wants any information about his existence in the early years, all she has to do is leaf through the album. It is proof. It is the confirmation of an existence. Laconically, Johannes recorded what his daughter did, where they took her, her state of health. Brief phrases, without comment. Like answers to a questionnaire. There are no impressions, feelings. Life is simplified, almost as if it were not there. Johannes notes: his daughter has never cried. She has not been rebellious, she behaves correctly. A proper infancy. All is on the surface. About himself, Johannes, two personal notes. A minor heart attack and the carcinoma. When his daughter was two, notes Johannes, her grandfather (he writes the grandfather's name and surname) died. At the cremation, many friends. His daughter shows herself to be nice and discovers everything. Johannes does not write "understands," but "discovers." So, the man observes his daughter. She must have been really well brought up and sweet, that little girl, about her grandfather's death. Perhaps even then Johannes was thinking about his own death and hoped that the girl would be nice to everyone. That she would be nice to the world. To grief. When she was still small, she had to leave Johannes. Children lose interest in their parents when they are left. They are not sentimental. They are passionate and cold. In a certain sense some people abandon affections, sentiments, as if they were things. With determination, without sorrow. They become strangers. Sometimes enemies. They are no longer creatures that have been abandoned, but those who mentally beat a retreat. And they go away. Toward a gloomy, fantastic, and wretched world. Yet at times they feign happiness. Like funambulists, they practice. Parents are not necessary. Few things are necessary. Some children look after themselves. The heart, incorruptible crystal. They learn to pretend. And pretence becomes the most active, the realest part, alluring as dreams. It takes the place of what we think is real. Perhaps that is all there is to it, some children have the gift of detachment.

Father and daughter stand before the ship. She looks like a naval vessel. The red star glitters on the funnel. I look immediately at the lettering *Proleterka*. Blackened, patches of rust, forgotten. Sovereign lettering. The dusk is falling. The ship is large, she hides the sun that is about to sink into the water. She is darkness, pitch, and mystery. A privateer built like a fortress, she has survived stormy weather and shipwreck. We go up the gangplank. The officers are waiting for us. We are the last. Johannes has trouble getting up, and an officer helps him. They show us the cabin. Small.

I would sleep there with Johannes. Two bunks, one above the other. I will have to sleep on top. The *Proleterka* puts out to sea at 1800 hours. She slips gently over the water. A raucous sound precedes our departure. A sound of farewell. There is no turning back. I look out of the porthole. I wonder how I shall manage to get out, to get into the sea, should I wish to slip away like Martin Eden.

I get changed. An hour's time in the dining room. On the deck the passengers are looking at the sunset. They cannot miss it. Johannes is watching the sunset too. By now it illuminates nothing anymore. Darkness is come, the voyage has begun. The first sunset will be followed by others, for fourteen days. The Guild people are sure that they have organized everything in the best possible way. Even the weather. A sailor invites the ladies and gentlemen to go into the dining room. One after the other, almost in silence, the passengers in line. My father and I are again the last. We have a corner table. Johannes reads the menu, chooses the wine. He greets his friends, I greet them with a tight-lipped smile. Muggy heat. The ship sails on serenely. The crystal chandelier sways slightly. Like a leisurely pendulum, moved by inertia. Johannes is dressed in dark colors. Impeccable. We have barely exchanged a word. The ladies are in evening dress, a few grudging décolletés. In the room a continuous, slow, persistent swaying. A calm, malign rhythm, as if the waves of the sea were crooning a lullaby before stupefying the passengers. The chandelier swings a little more. It casts its light on the passengers and then leaves them in shadow, only to return faster. The room rises and falls. The flowers on the table move at irregular intervals. They slip away and then return to their place. Johannes distant, absent, elsewhere. Dessert, trifle. During dessert the force of the sea increases. I ask Johannes's leave to get up. Outside, a raging wind. Shadows move frenetically. They are the sailors. I breathe in the sublime nocturnal solitude. The bad weather. And the danger. I do not think of Johannes. Of giving him my arm and helping him. Nothing matters at that moment.

I cannot keep my feet. After a few minutes a sailor grabs me and hurls me in front of my cabin. The crew had ordered all the passengers to remain in their cabins. They managed to finish the trifle.

The *Proleterka* has changed course. She is heading for Zara. A sailor, perhaps the same one who grabbed me, was seriously injured during the night. The following morning he was on a stretcher. I caress his face, I give his hand a squeeze. The stretcher is lowered onto a motor launch. I should like to leave the ship too. The captain salutes.

The passengers are fine. We are in the dining room for breakfast. Two days sailing before we arrive in Greece. Today all is calm. I do not see Johannes; it is as if he has disappeared. Like the storm. Some passengers are stretched out on the deck chairs. Me too. I think of nothing. Nothingness is the stuff of thought. Beings, autonomous voices, memories dredged up, follow the lapping of the water. Nothingness is not empty. As if fallen from the talons of a bird of prey in flight, thoughts drop into our mind when we are convinced that we are not thinking. Johannes appears. A good, sad smile. He asks if I am well, if I am *zufrieden*. As if it were our obsession, father and daughter. That of not being sad, of concealing the sadness that has left its mark on us for no reason. This voyage is important to him. Before leaving, I had thought that the destination was unimportant to me. The journey to Greece was a part of my education. It is our first voyage and it looks like the last. Johannes, improbably, is a stranger to me. My father. No intimacy. But a bond that precedes our existences. Acquaintances amid complete extraneousness.

We are in the dining room at the usual hour. I went down to the cabin to change. I have few clothes, almost all the same. Does Johannes undress, before going to bed? I have never seen him in a swimsuit. I have never seen his legs. One night has gone by, I have not perceived his presence. The abolition of the body. It is the second day and everything is repeated. Johannes greets his friends. I greet them too. Johannes introduced me to his friends when I was a child. They criticized their friend's only daughter. Sometimes children have a premonitory notion of social standing. Of appearances. If one is accepted or not. I was not accepted, but they were my father's friends. In a certain sense, although he was a solitary man, Johannes was a part of their world. But not his daughter. My father Johannes was part of it by birth, by status. My father's friend and his family were my childhood judges. And their house. And the windows. The objects. The objects, the judges. Their rich house. Perhaps I had no liking for those rich people who used to invite my father and me to their homes. They know that my father was once rich like them. I knew that Johannes had been rich. Like them. Now no longer. They are simple, easygoing, which is how one behaves when one has everything. One is indulgent. An acrimonious indulgence. This is what I used to think when I observed them as a child. Observe and keep quiet. Johannes's daughter was not simple, nor indulgent, nor easygoing. She did not go along with their proprietorial simplicity, the haughty mildness of her father's great friend. "You'll have to keep an eye on her, with all those sailors." My father's friend looks up from beneath gold half-moon spectacles. He appraises his friend's daughter. He has thick white gleaming hair. The air of the master ready to listen, not to concede. His face is ruddy. His wife deprives herself of everything, even of herself. She has nibbled at her body, leaving the long teeth, when she shows them. She is withered, puritan, and castigatory. She was the first person to observe Johannes's daughter through the lens of contempt. She is abysmally polite. Hair gathered up into a lump, a chignon at the nape of the neck. Eyes dripping rapacious charity. Always kind. Those who condemn us are understanding. Like her. She understands sinners. A savage fury at sinners, repressed, without explosions and without remission. A highly sorrowful understanding. She is outraged by the ills of humanity. And she embodies that outrage in a vainglorious restraint. In her tone of voice, bane, complaint, and acceptance. To Johannes, a man so old and alone, who shows joy at having a daughter, she intimates that joy is merely an illusion, that joy is dangerous, it must be rooted out. Joy must be transformed into suffering. She pities Johannes. His daughter, while they are in their house, says: "Let's go."

My father's fine friends are also collectors. When they invited us to dinner, the wife would sit at the head of the table toward the wall, beneath a picture. She joins her hands, eyelids lowered, murmuring. Johannes's daughter does not pray. I do not thank the Lord for the food that he and she give us. I do not thank you, she says to herself. Before the repast of the righteous begins, the woman's face glazes over, vacuous. This is her prayer. The wife thanks

17

the Lord with a bleak and rigid expression. As she draws nearer the Lord, her blood freezes, pallor flows into her face. As if the grace were a request for forgiveness, *mea culpa* if there is something to eat.

Every time, I would wait for the moment in which she offered thanks with her hands contracted in prayer. I savor all her gestures. And after dessert I would wait for her to thank the Lord again. Then one went into the lounge. More pictures. Collectors have pictures everywhere. They do not let the walls breathe. Armchairs. View over the lake. View over the lawn. The two friends talk. One laughs, the other less. When the Spanish maid passes, Johannes gives her a tip. That was the custom. And pralines for the lady. "Take her nothing," I say to Johannes. The friend, when he speaks to my father, uses a name that sounds Hungarian. When I went to call my father by that name he asked me not to. Perhaps only his friend has the right to call him that. Since they were students. A thing between initiates. His friend had a name too, but it was to do with the goods produced by his factory. Johannes no longer had a factory and therefore he had only a nickname. Of one who no longer possesses anything. Save for a daughter, which is not an asset. Johannes and I no longer have anything. His best friend knows this. His wife: the Lord has given, the Lord has taken away. Not from them. I knew this with a certain precision since they put me in the care of a lady who agreed to take me in.

House with garden, view over the lake. In the garden the children play. The children said: "You have lost everything." They sang it to the sound of a march. Happy, exhilarated, exultant. The pure ferocity of the joy that manifests itself in annunciation. In the annunciation of financial ruin. Broke, broke, broke, they chanted. Johannes's parents have lost their fortune, consequently Johannes and his daughter have too. The children know the economic situation of their schoolmates, especially that of Johannes's daughter. Broke, broke, broke, they sound like frogs croaking, louder and louder. They were the little relatives, the children of relatives, cousins; they were part of the family. So they know everything. Broke, broke, broke, their mothers must have sung in the kitchens as, radiant, they baked the cakes. A chorus of general satisfaction.

The war was not long over, although the war that was elsewhere had not caused them any hardship. But they had filled the cellars with provisions.

You enter the garden through an iron gate with sharp spikes. There were roses, camellias, fruit trees, magnolias, trimmed hedges, and a greenhouse with lemon trees. And palms. The mistress of the house would cut the camellias and, still warm from the spring sunshine, she would lay them in a cardboard box. "Gently," she would say. I had to wrap them up in tissue paper. Like living creatures, those flowers with the rosy petals, barely bruised, sometimes white, or streaked with red, were laid down for departure. Closed beneath a label and an address. Perhaps they were crying out with pain, but no one heard them. They were sent to her lady friends. With the passing years, the lady ran out of those. She survived. She took roses and camellias to the cemetery. I used to look at the stones with the names of unknown people engraved upon them. I would fantasize about those names, the portraits in the corridor and in the rooms of the house. Sometimes I would sit in a room beside a large mirror with a gilt frame. After having opened the window, I would look for a long time at the finest portrait in the house: the reflection of the garden. The plants drew nearer in the mirror, while the green of the leaves moved by the breeze and by the brilliance of the light formed a primitive landscape, the very essence of nature. As if the truth let itself be filtered by a mirror. By a reflection. In winter the camellias rested beneath a pyramid of dry leaves and twigs. As soon as the season grew milder, the mistress of the house would go to visit them to see if they had reawakened. I was her assistant gardener. Her name is Orsola. She is my mistress. She is the mother of my mother, of her who had been Johannes's wife. Johannes has to ask her permission if he wants to visit me. We do not want visitors. Sometimes Orsola says: "Johannes has my permission to visit his daughter." They use the polite form of address. And the term of the visit is final.

After a few months, Johannes's daughter was in primary one. She learns to sing. The father of one of the children dies. The most unrelenting member of the chorus, the boy was seven years old. "*Du hast deinen Vater verloren*," chants Johannes's daughter. You have lost your father. The boy has a melancholy look. The vision of his father darkens his iris. The words pass before his eyes as if on a screen, without touching him. "Yes, yes," says the boy absently, distantly. "You've lost your father." It is a sing-song. The rigidity of the boy's look has something remote about it. This egged Johannes's daughter on. The boy does not react. He replies calmly, monotonous and sorrowful: "Yes, yes." Almost as if grief were made of patience, wisdom, confirmation of the irremediable. "You've lost your father." "Yes," repeats the boy, like an automaton. An atonal, bleak yes. The boy shifts his gaze elsewhere. Not to see the words anymore. He replies no longer. In that moment I sensed a wound, a painful spasm. The perception of what it means to hurt. To inflict pain deliberately. The cognition of pain. I was illuminated by the boy's wordless suffering. I take his hand. An inert hand, which accepts mine. I try to apologize, I do not succeed. Awareness is the only forgiveness, I think, which can be attained.

Orsola is a widow. Always has been, it seems. In the house and garden, the past. The past in the rooms, in the objects. The rooms facing the interior, almost on the road to darkness. In the turret that, half asleep, overlooks the lake. Every evening I obey Orsola. I must close all the shutters. I close the eyelids of the house. The turret has no shutters. It is a reliquary of physiognomies. The portraits of Johannes's parents are stacked up on the floor. In costume. This is how I met them. The woman with the bonnet. A starched, tight bodice, meticulous pleats that look like cannulae made of glass. Of glass the whites of her eyes. A patina of ebony over her complexion. She would get darker still, I thought, like something unfinished that must manifest itself. Even her eyes have become darker. She is a woman from the North. Watchful eyes. She is posing for her son who will look at her when she is no more. Her smile is pensive. The smile of farewell. She has decided to abandon her little city whose river ran red at sunset, they say, with the tears of the glacier. They sold the factory. For their sick son. To offer him a temperate, mild place, a house and the vegetation of the South where the invalid could stay in the garden for long periods. And have the impression of living. Where his face could float through the palms, the magnolias, and the eucalyptus trees, not like the reflection of a dead thing.

In a short time they lost everything. The creditors called in. And the bank people. Johannes's parents wait together with their portraits for everything to end. She in the *Tracht*. He in the black suit, the starched shirt front, his eyes vacuous and severe. A tenuous sky blue. They seem to return to antiquity. Centuries distant in the gaze of a little girl. They await the end. Dispossession. The place in the South, the one that was to be the salvation of the invalid son, is ruin. Calm ruin. As if calm were imposed by violence. Johannes's twin brother's wheelchair stands motionless in front of the house, his gaze is trained on his parents as they prepare the inventory for the sale of the furniture, the paintings, the carpets. A gaze that is fixed as long as he manages to keep his eyes open. Now, he thinks, his parents are doing what he would have wished. They are taking the furniture out of the lounge, and thus he will no longer have barriers. Away too with the divan, on which he has never sat. Those two sat on it, dressed as in the portraits, and spoke in low, soft voices. They are suffering. They have no comfort. He is merely cold. They are suffering, he is cold. What more can one wish for. Stagnation and the will of the Lord.

Very little is left. Almost everything has been packed up. The big black mantel clock with the columns still marks the hour. Apparently immobile. This is what the twin liked, the hands that love neither the past nor the future. The hands point at the numbers as if out of caprice. In the end, even the clock falls silent. Carried off like a mummy. Others would look at the face of the black clock with the columns and listen to the chimes, which spoke to the twin with an oriental sound, almost a voice.

The nurse coddled the twin, treating him like an infant. This is not good. It is offensive. "The gentleman is not to worry," she used to say. "It's nothing. He will start talking and laughing again like before." The twin grows ever calmer. Like the things that allow themselves to be carried off. He tries to get up from the wheelchair. The house in the South will be removed from the earth by a thrust of the spade.

On the floor, in the turret, a small picture. A black man standing in front of a cornfield. He is smoking a pipe. He looks straight ahead. He has watched the invalid son of the white gentlefolk grow up. He is part of the family. An inexorable, bewitched melancholy links the portraits to Johannes's twin brother. Orsola was reluctant to take in the three pictures that had escaped the auction. Genealogy spoke to me, I was looking for something that might have lingered on in my father's features. What remains in him of his twin brother? Perhaps the twin lives on in Johannes. And perhaps he makes him limp, in order to put limits on Johannes's vital mechanisms. To re-establish a kind of divine justice.

I manage to decipher the quasi-glacial affection that Orsola felt for me. I do not know if I felt affection for her. Certainly it was the most intense relationship I had ever had. I would sit on her right at the table in the frescoed dining room. French windows gave onto the pergola of wild grape. Facing her was her portrait with the children. With whom did I sit at table before? It was another gap. I had no memories of the period before when I learned to write. Sometimes a person's existence starts late. An absent life, or a nonexistence, can last a long time. Is it an anomaly? Perhaps a lack of images. I can describe Orsola's dining-room table, I cannot describe previous tables or rooms. A few names linger on, the feel of certain objects, wood, the contours of a room. Orsola is the guide to the images. The portraits, my partners in conversation. She gives me orders. I would obey. She bids me goodnight in the corridor and goes up the stairs. To the top floor. My room is downstairs.

I have a wooden bed, a bedside table, a wardrobe, a mirror that can accommodate at least five people, a desk for my homework. Sometimes I would stay awake, to convince myself that I was sleeping in my room. I would draw Orsola. And I took possession of her. Her effigy is mine. I wondered when she would turn me out. By day she gave nothing away. I was distant from her, as she was from me. In a certain sense, a perfect union. In the cellar, her gardening tools. And mine. The present. Every day the flowers have to be looked after. In the turret, the past. Some cupboards and rooms in the attic have padlocks. They are the places where the dead leave their things. And perhaps come to take them back. Where do the crates come from? From Buenos Aires, says Orsola. She had no further wish to open them since they arrived by sea in Genoa. As a young woman, Orsola lived in Buenos Aires. Her children were born there. My mother and her two sisters as well. We have scant news of them. They are grasping and diffident. When the mail came, I would check it; if there were letters from the two sisters, I would throw them away. I think Orsola knew that. Besides, she too would make Johannes's letters disappear, the ones with the *pro Juventute* stamps. And the parcels with presents. It would happen in the corridor, where the mail was laid on a tallboy. Where the black telephone, an antiquated rectangular box, was attached to the wall. It was almost never used. One does not make telephone calls. Johannes used to call once a week, always at the same time, seven-forty p.m. Orsola asked him not to call, if it was not strictly necessary. Now she has my company. When she talks to me, she reflects. She reflects on my future. I ask nothing. I do not want to know. Johannes arrives. We have an appointment in a hotel. Johannes leaves again. Orsola and I are alone. She asks if I was glad to see my father. Yes, thank you.

Orsola had a son who wrote letters from a sanatorium in Davos. It seemed as if it was the tuberculosis that kept him alive. He would spend hours on the veranda of the sanatorium, daydreaming. Before him, the mountains. Silent shadows run across virgin snow. And crows. One flies very close to the window. They look at each other. The crow promises to return the following day. The doctors give orders that the boy who dreams must not be disturbed. As he slowly died, he dreamed he had his twentieth birthday.

The weather was almost always fair. The winters terse. Sometimes I can go up to Orsola's room. A woman brushes her long white hair. Then she gathers it up. In Buenos Aires a *dueña* used to dress her. She would pull her corsets tight. While her husband sought his fortune. She is my Argentinean mistress. I think she comes from afar. From unknown worlds, whence perhaps she would like to return. A part of her eyes has remained in Tierra del Fuego. She cannot know that the girl she took in would like to return there where she is now. In the house with the garden and her. The girl who has no past. Orsola treats me like an adult. Like a peer. Obedience does not mean subordination. I close all the shutters. I do not open them in the mornings. A continuous closing. I close the days. Closing is order. It is a form of detachment. An ephemeral preparation for death. An exercise. It was entirely natural that that woman and the garden corresponded to the vision of a happy land. How much time did I still have at my disposal? The curtains at the windows are fragile, almost dust. And she, the mistress, looks like a white plaster bust.

In the garden of the house that had belonged to Johannes's parents, a glacial stillness. One cannot rule out the notion that some places may find new owners hard to bear. Those who came afterward had merely intruded on the suffering that had settled there. Objects rebel sometimes. Objects, like rooms, think. Perhaps nothing can be completely destroyed. Just as nothing is a victory.

I often heard talk of crimes. Orsola talked at length about the trial of a banker who had killed his son's wife. She knew him. The owners of villas usually know one another. He was the one who had bought Johannes's parents' house. And then, not far from Orsola's house, lives a man who killed his mother. He moved there only recently. A mild and sweet man. He did not know why he had done it. His mouth was affected by a slight tic. They sentenced him to seven years in prison. He got out early for good behavior. I met him after he had served his sentence.

Johannes protected that man. He almost seemed grateful to him. With him, he used a tone of voice that was different from the one he used with his friends in the Guild. More indulgent, knowing. Almost loving. Why? I wondered. The man looked younger than his age, about sixty. At least ten years younger. Suave, with a trace of disquietude. Killing his mother must have rejuvenated him. He had strangled her. It had all happened so fast. Before he knew it, his mother was lifeless and he called Johannes. And Johannes had rushed straight over. He took the tram from the Bahnhofstrasse. He looks absently out of the window. It is winter. He did not take off his dark gray hat. In winter his eyes become evanescent. He keeps his stick beside him. After a few stops, he gets off. He does not understand why, but he feels light. Relieved. The city on the lake looks more beautiful to him. He knows the streets near the Kunsthaus, he feels tenderness for those districts where he spent the unhappiest years of his life. With his wife. It had been really nice of her to leave. To leave him. Johannes observes the houses. He passes in front of the house where he used to live. He is vaguely touched, a little, on looking at the windows that conceal the rooms where his solitary life began. Where he no longer heard the voice of his daughter. He looks up toward the terrace on the top floor. The little one had sat there with her rabbit. She said she wanted to throw herself off the terrace with the rabbit, then she let herself be photographed as she hugged the rabbit on the edge of the terrace. She did not lose her balance. She never lost it. Like her father. They have always been able to perceive the exceedingly fine line between equilibrium and desperation. Johannes cannot tear himself away. The murderer is waiting for him, he thinks. Yet he lingers, looking at where adversity had passed through, or perhaps lodged itself in the impeccable shutters and frames of a house occupied by others. His wife took everything: the girl too. Since then, he can have her on loan. Shortly afterward, Johannes would lose his family fortune too. The girl's mother managed to get away before. Before the ineluctable end of a fortune. Now, in order to see his daughter for a few days more, Johannes has to ask permission, which is denied him. When his daughter grows up, perhaps he will be able to stay with her. But when she grows up, he will be no more. He knows this with precision. With this final thought, he heads off for the murderer's house.

He is the only person that Johannes introduced me to outside his circle of friends. A murderer. It was when Orsola gave my father permission to come to visit me. Together we went to the new house with a small garden owned by the man who had killed his mother. I could not stop myself from looking at him with curiosity. I wanted to catch something in his aspect that might reveal him. I found no particular trace. He was a resigned man, of an almost obsessive mildness. The entire room was docile. A docile bunch of flowers, docile and mannered pictures on the walls. Fussy chairs, a table with an ornamental doily in the middle. The man was not at his ease. Not because of Johannes, who had been his defender. But because of the little girl. He avoided my gaze. I wanted to know why one kills. If such a terribly mild man had killed his mother, he must have felt an exasperation so sweet that it triggered the frenzy. Orsola is not sweet. So she cannot be a murderess.

Orsola was displeased by Johannes's taking me to the house of a murderer. I try to tell her that it had been a very interesting encounter. He has your father to thank, she said, if he spent such a short time in prison. Johannes speaks to the murderer with benevolence. It seemed that he knew him profoundly. And understood him. "You know," I say to Johannes, "that man wants to escape. Escape from freedom." Johannes smiles. Sorrowful. Orsola forbade Johannes to come to visit me. So I ask Johannes what would happen to me, at seven years of age, if I killed Orsola. Nothing. Would I go to prison? No.

Orsola and I are alone in the big house. She does not want me to play with the other children in the street. She says I must not speak to strangers. They can be dangerous. Near the church there is a hedge, beyond the hedge brushwood and darkness. There, not far from home, they found a little girl who had been killed. Orsola keeps repeating that they have found a girl, killed. Of my age. One morning someone rang the doorbell. The corridor was flooded with light. On the glass of the door the extremely tall shadow of a man.

The man wanted to sell religious pamphlets. I screamed. Orsola scolds me. "Isn't he a stranger, then?" I ask. Who would have grabbed me in order to deposit me beyond the hedge. Orsola is ashamed of me. She thinks I see murderers everywhere. It is the influence of Johannes, who took me to a murderer's house. I dare to ask her if after serving the sentence you are still a murderer. She makes no reply. It seemed to me that the subject irritated her. Or that it was not the right moment. There are times when you can say what you think or ask questions, and others when you can't. These are the so-called wrong moments. And since the wrong moments fill up the hours, you end up not asking any more. She did not forgive if one made a mistake. In not forgiving she was magnanimous, tolerant, equable.

In the happy land, Johannes's daughter begins to fall ill. Johannes wants to go to visit her. Orsola says she must have no excitement. At school I am doing badly. I avoid the portraits in the turret. Orsola does not want Johannes to give me presents. I must have no excitement. I am in bed. Orsola's periwinkle-blue eyes look at me from on high. I am fine, I tell Orsola. I tell her to switch off the light. I must close all the shutters. The windows and the rooms have to sleep. Johannes's album records his daughter's illness. It is not stated what illness it is. "Another crisis." No comment. Perhaps he thought it was a nausea typical of difficult children. Visitors forbidden. Even my schoolmates. Who never came. I am served boiled rice. I get used to the attacks of nausea. They emulate my thoughts. I was deferring the moment. By then I was sure. Orsola would invite me to leave. When she comes into the room, it is authority manifesting itself. My reputation, like my marks in school, is low. I had become weak. I needed to live in advance what was going to happen. The garden smothers the house. The vegetation is luxuriant in its impassiveness. For months, the room and I savor the mephitic air of a suffering that has still to come to pass. Orsola, elegant in her silk dress, says: "The windows need opening." Certainly, I think, amid the docility of the embroidered sheets between which I seem to have been pressed too, suffering does not have a good smell.

All the rooms know. Likewise the portraits. Ancestors who do not favor a better lot for their successors. For the children. Perhaps Johannes's twin in his wheelchair went from garden to garden trampling over the fate of Johannes's daughter. Objects and predecessors, names no longer uttered, a genealogy of images was against me. I stand listening to the news, the decision of my departure. Orsola's voice comes from a chair behind the desk. "It is for your own good." "And Johannes?" "Your father will do as we decide." It is for my own good. A venomous expression. But it sounds good. I know that that expression has never boded any good. Since then it has worsened my condition as a minor. You ought to watch your back when listening to diktats of this kind. When you are a hostage to good. A prisoner of good. The good of the people. Expressions typical of dictatorships. I leave the house with a suitcase and my schoolbag. I have been consigned to others.

For my own good.

Auf Hoher See. Another two days of sailing on the high seas. The ship will not put in at Malta. I do not mind if, on account of the forces of nature, I shall not see something. A day lost. We ought to have docked in Malta at seven in the morning: at seven thirty a visit to the city, on foot. The visit would have lasted until twelve. At one o'clock all aboard ship, in the dining room. The ladies and gentlemen of the Guild in the dining room without having seen Malta. They are silent. Impatient. Doggedly they read the menu. Johannes reads the menu. It is written in French. Langouste en bellevue. The extras are paid for in Yugoslavian dinars. From the corner table, I observe the langoustines of the Guild. Their ruddy complexions. Johannes greets his friends. If people want to be reached by telegram, they must give the address of the ship: *Proleterka*. Johannes's wife, no longer a wife, sends a telegram to the command of the *Proleterka*. Text: "Je vous prie de bien vouloir surveiller votre fille." Please be so good as to look after your daughter. They wrote to each other in French, like the menu. They use the polite form of address. Perhaps when they lived together they spoke in German too. She was the one who gave permission for the voyage. After many refusals. I am grateful to her for that. Johannes is refused everything. He is allowed only what the law has established. The only favor granted is the trip to Greece. And it is thanks to this extraordinary concession that for fourteen days Johannes's daughter has been able to frequent her closest relative, her father. By virtue of this wholly unexpected permission she found herself in the midst of a crew. There was little time to get to know Johannes. Then everything has to finish. In fourteen days. It is not known why his former wife agreed to that voyage. Perhaps she wanted to do him a good turn, for the first and last time. They have told her that Johannes would not live much longer. Orsola was against it. Not living much longer doesn't cut any ice with her.

For the friends of the Guild, Johannes's wife was "the Italian woman." They had met thanks to Johannes's mother, when once she chanced to pass by a villa with a garden. She rang the doorbell. The woman was wearing a *Tracht*, the costume of her area, the Aargau. The skirt was full, dark red, soot and silk. The bodice in black damask. She introduced herself in a low, almost hoarse voice. She took the liberty of asking who was playing the piano. Standing there at the door, she listened to a Chopin nocturne as if she were listening to the *Landhelmi*, the sound of the alpenhorn. They introduced her to the pianist. The stranger's gaze alighted attentive and unwavering on the young woman. When she went back home, she told her husband: "I have found a wife for our son Johannes." A few months later she contracted the marriage.

That visit aroused the resentment of one of Johannes's fiancée's sisters on account of the good fortune that had fallen to the other. For the family was wealthy, and the future husband pandered to his fiancée's every whim.

And she had had no need to look for a husband, they had come to take her, to beg her to agree to the marriage. By the will of the Heavenly Father. Merely because that day she had been playing the piano. Without the will of the Heavenly Father, that vestige of the Aargau would never have entered the house, the sister had thought to console herself. But she could not manage to resign herself to the idea that the Heavenly Father dispensed gifts and not grief. She looked idly out of the window. The lake is calm. Flecked with pink. Her thoughts are calm. In her hands she clutches a little china cup as if it were a little skull. She had painted it herself. Tiny pink and sky-blue flowers on a white background. She had painted twelve teacups and twelve coffee cups. They were her wedding present to her sister. She gave her only six of them. She detested her, and to amuse herself she painted the leaves too. To amuse herself she added some gold. And in gold her name.

Johannes's wife, my mother, used to play the piano. When I was invited to stay with her, I would listen to her for hours. Perhaps this is why I am attracted to the sound of the piano. Like the unknown woman in the *Tracht*, if I hear the sound of a piano, I follow it. The sound of the piano represents all that I have not had. I used to hear it playing when I was very small, when she was still married to Johannes. Then that sound ceased. The rooms fell silent. I hated that silence, without realizing it. The silence received from a man and a woman who were leaving each other and who had disposed of their daughter's life absolutely. To this day, when I listen to the piano, I am seized by a violent emotion. I do not know what it is, but my mind goes back toward something beautiful, distant, destroyed.

Simply because Johannes's wife, my mother, deceived me. By playing the piano, she spoiled my feeling for music.

When I return to the places where she used to play the piano, buried places by now, I still hear the sound. I accord her a presence that is there no longer. With precision, the sound of the piano, a mental and visual sound, utters words of death and condemnation. Now the Steinway is locked up in a room. It is a prisoner. Only I can have it released. Or let someone play it. The portrait of Johannes's mother is in the room with the Steinway. The canvas has a vertical tear in the middle of her forehead. His mother had chanced to hear the young lady playing the piano. Sometimes objects meet again.

I am almost convinced that she, Johannes's wife, plays the piano in the closed room. That she comes to visit me, that the dead do exactly the same things they did when alive. Just as Johannes waited for permission to see me, waited for permission to meet his daughter. And today Johannes is waiting for me. Once I happened to see him in a chalet (he had been dead for some time). Outside one window it was snowing and outside the opposite window it was not snowing. Johannes is standing. He has been waiting for hours while it snows at one side of the room but not at the other. I ask him: "Why didn't you call me?" He replies that he did not know that he had to call me, he was waiting. And as he waits, he vanishes. He and I are in waiting rooms. Not like Johannes's wife, who had passion and kindness, impatience. Johannes likes the vivacity, the occasionally darkling joy of his wife. Who acts out her temperament with that cold and polite man. His wife managed to make him laugh, later only to regret having made him laugh. There are women who have a tendency, almost a vocation, to punish men. They have an ecumenical capacity for doing so. Pleasure and punishment combined. It is not out of any reasoning, it is out of a pure impulse to be spiteful. It goes back for generations in the women of Johannes's wife's family.

They were women who ruled households and persons. Long-lived. After having raised their children, flowers and cards took first place. Flowers would become an obsession. Likewise diseases and parasites. Which eat into leaves and petals. But their flowers and leaves were almost always healthy, unlike the gardens of others, which were diseased.

There might have been a war on somewhere else, and there was. They were concerned most of all about the flowers. I am suspicious of anyone who grows flowers, the way the women of Johannes's wife's family did. The only one who was not totally devoted to flowers was Johannes's wife. More to cards. And far more, because it was a true, immensely grand passion, to the piano. I suppose because it took her mind off the world. She used to play for seven hours a day. Then silence. The women of that family had an autistic passion for camellias, roses, and nothing else. Scant liking for human beings. We found this reprehensible. I do not know why I say "we."

Perhaps simply because I think of Johannes's twin brother. There is no one at my side who can judge or merely observe women who think exclusively of their flowers. Fanatical in their care for them. A passion like that is voracious, secret. It only seems like a nice thing. Taking an interest in nature. But instead they harbor a profound resentment, a visceral resentment toward the world, toward existence. Toward men. Toward the male gender. Toward Johannes. They have tried everything in order to transmit that predisposition to Johannes's daughter as well. The women of her family, of Johannes's wife's family, are no more. They too continue doing the same things they did in life. I think they send me bags of the finest quality earth to promote the growth of any shoot. To promote the growth of any feelings of hatred for the male gender. For Johannes.

Sometimes I sit down beside the piano. "Play." I look at the keys, some of them yellowed. "Play, I beg you." I close the window because I do not want the sound to go out. Other times, in previous years, suddenly someone would play the piano. But this did not happen in one room only. It happened in the open too. Thus, for no reason, in the countryside, the sound would come coiling out. Then, suddenly, it would cease. As if the keys had fallen out. Far more difficult when I found myself in the room with the piano. The Steinway & Sons and I. She had bought it in New York. And it had traveled on an ocean liner. She too traveled on the *Andrea Doria* together with the piano. I remained ashore. To imagine a sea voyage, a vegetation I would never see. To look at all the things my mother, the pianist, had left me or sent me. A frock. Another frock. Another frock again. To go where? She sent the frocks to a girl who did not wear frocks, because she wore a uniform. A school uniform.

Many years have passed, now the Steinway is in my possession. I can do what I wish with it. I sit beside it and I say: "I can burn you." Then I look at it. No one dusts my Steinway. The pedals remain shiny. It lives in a small frescoed room.

A room that was waiting unbeknownst to me for the piano that arrived from New York. I should like to keep it open. Perhaps, when I call her to tell her to play it, she prefers it to be open.

In New York I even went to see the Steinway & Sons shop. The shop seemed slumbrous in the half-light. A tall, polite gentleman, dressed in dark colors, speaks in a low voice. I had the feeling that the shop was a funeral home for pianos. It made quite an impression on me. It looks like a shop that the have-nots cannot enter. Where only those who belong to a very high social stratum may enter. And elegant people. With a musical culture. I think that she, my mother, must have been elegant when she bought the Steinway. A French outfit, Patou or Givenchy. A shyness that was fairly sure of itself. She could enter that shop. I, on visiting it, or on feigning interest in the pianos, was ill at ease. I asked a price. I should not have done that. My mother certainly did not ask the price of her, and now my, Steinway & Sons. It must have been toward the end of spring when she bought it. And she was certainly wearing a really beautiful silk dress, gauzy and light. Sometimes clothes give an accurate idea of a person's spiritual traits. The Steinway shop was very large with subdued lighting. My mother's dress, the customer's dress, gave off an arcane light, cold and silvery. The assistant, or the proprietor, of the shop must have been captivated by the *charme* of that customer. Even though the shop was self-important, almost wary of selling or giving explanations of its Steinway & Sons pianos. This was how it struck me when I visited it, the way I would have visited a museum. A museum for a few. More than two people cannot go in to look at those marvelous simulacra. Those pianos that, like mine, in the little room, look as if they might play from one moment to the next.

The customer must have given her New York address. Of a house that I would not have seen. And at the same time she asked for information about shipping. I do not think that the Steinway suffered on the sea. At that time, it was not yet a sentient being. It became one by living with the pianist. Now the pianist does not show herself. Or perhaps, when she comes, I turn the other way. I did not know that I would live in a house where there is a music room. It was a coincidence. It was the Steinway's wish to come to stay where it is now. In a little room frescoed with musical motifs. A long time ago. Long before I was born. Time is insignificant. Isn't it, Steinway? But the bond you share with the pianist is not insignificant. Nor is your wish to stay with someone who has blood ties with the pianist. And who prepared this room for you.

You do not want me to touch your keys yet. My fingers are unfamiliar to you. That slight hint of carnality. But I am sitting beside you. I watch over you. In the first years I always kept the door closed. I wanted to be sure that no one came in. You alone, locked in. Now no longer. Now I allow you more freedom. And at the same time I allow myself more freedom too. I have become wiser. Before, if I felt resentment, it seeped into my veins, my eyes, my thoughts. An insomniac resentment. You know what insomnia is like. It is unpleasant. It is awful. For all is presence. Nocturnal presences. In the silent hours, when insomnia stalks through the rooms, in your room it is freezing. And so I sit down beside you. Your keys are really cold. Then, dawn at the window. I wonder if the pianist awakes. You are a horse with golden hoofs. What does the dawn bring to you and me? Have you already chosen your next home? You tell me that there is time, that I must not be in a hurry. I am in no hurry, Steinway, I would like to carry on like this, you and I, in the little room with the ceiling in the colors of Pompeii. It is like a gentle blaze, gentle flames, celestial color of fire.

One still, sunny afternoon. Johannes's daughter visits a squalid room. A green night-light over the door. Like an eye on a perch. Ever vigilant. Day and night. Even more luminous at night. It sheds its light of brute compassion over a bed. It is the room of segregation. It is the room of my mistress, the mistress of the house and of the garden. The shadows are green, as is she, Orsola, and the sheets. She is wrapped in a shroud of mold. She is over a hundred years old, exhausted by not dying. Exhausted by reclusion. Her daughters had deposited her in there, waiting for the end. Which was taking a long time. Now Johannes's daughter is sitting beside the bed. The hands of the woman, of the woman that Johannes's daughter had loved, flutter nervously on the sheets. She wants to make knots. To escape. And to return to her garden. To her home. Johannes's daughter is silent. Like her beloved mistress many years before, she looks at the green night-light that gives no peace. She ought to say something, perhaps something consoling, to the woman who wants nothing else but to die.

Orsola sees only the green light. It is the most luminous thing that appears to her. More than memories. The eye on its perch has stolen her gaze. It has stripped her memories of color. Sometimes she thinks about her only son, in the sanatorium in Davos. When he was admitted, he was not very ill. But every day, slowly, slowly, he grew more tired. He wanted a dinner jacket. He writes to Orsola, his mother, saying that he wants the dinner jacket. He wants the tailor in the sanatorium. He has been invited to a ball. By an English girl. Not very beautiful, he says in the letter, she looks like a boy. In the sanatorium, her son thought of nothing but his dinner jacket. Orsola tried to recall her son's face. Since her memories no longer have any color, they have lost consistency. She cannot manage to see even the black of the dinner jacket and the white of the shirt. The night-light has scythed down all her memories. The dinner jacket remains, like a relic. They sent it back to her, when her son died. Now she, like her son, has a single prayer. As the dinner jacket was for him, so extinction is for her. No one wants to answer that prayer. Useless prayer. Her son did not manage to go to the ball. He was happy about the tailor who took his measurements. He was happy when he had the last fitting for the jacket. The final rehearsal of his life. He could bear to forego desperation.

The funeral cortège passes in front of the garden. It stops for three minutes. They have dressed Orsola in a silk suit and a blouse with a jabot. She is certainly not looking at the garden. She no longer wanted anything to do with earthly things, starting with herself and her daughters. Considerate and criminal. They did not dare to hasten something that she had desired for years. She would like to have seen one daughter again, Johannes's former wife, by then another man's wife, always far away. The first two were too close. Close to her death throes. One with red hair, the other with a turban on her head. They said

that their mother had had difficulty in dying, that she had
had to struggle. They said this in a rush of enthusiasm,
almost as if a match had been played out on that deathbed.
Orsola tried to suffocate the breath of life as if it were the
devil. She tried with all her might, according to what her
daughters said, to emerge victorious from the battle against
life. Despite her writhing, she could not find peace. She
grew feebler and feebler. The consumption gave her no
respite. Exhausted by the final struggle, she still had fits
of impatience and irritation. It was as if death had amused
itself by playing hard to get despite those periwinkle blue
eyes, the most beautiful eyes it had ever encountered. Yet
it wanted to be the one who doused them.

It is night. One of Orsola's daughters is playing cards. "I
don't hold it against her for making me wait so long." It
would be unspeakable to reprove one's own mother for
taking a long time to die. She, the daughter with the red
hair, does not have these disagreeable thoughts. Even
though she has waited a long time. To become the mistress
at last. "I no longer have any obligations." No one listens to
her, the house is uninhabited. There is only her, the new
mistress. She likes conversation. Even though it is often a
monologue. Every day she had gone to visit her mother in
that dignified and squalid place. She can well say that now:
she chose that truly squalid place. She knows how to take
care of herself, the new mistress; like not falling down, the
number one hazard. In the kitchen a notice with the list
of hazards. By playing cards she avoids hazards. By playing
cards she avoids falling and breaking her femur. Now that
she is the mistress of everything. Not everything. There
is another heir. Johannes's former wife. The new mistress

has only one thought in her head: may she not return, may her sister never return again. Cupboards and rooms are locked. She, the owner, keeps the bunch of keys, like a jailer. It is a vocation, that of the jailer. She does the rounds of the property. She curses her sister, who is younger than she. Her sister has more time to return. To demand what belongs to her. She is an heir just like her. And one day she might turn up at the house. Which is her house too. The third sister has passed on, in an Alpine cemetery. Now the heiress to half plays cards. Solitaire.

In November, on All Souls' Day, she is a happy woman. It was a day she awaited with impatience. "I'm off to visit my dead," she used to say. She set off proud and gloomy along the lakeshore. With her chrysanthemums. They have a mask, she thinks, ochre and violet, crimson and black, black and the color of her hair. So she might as well cut a lock of hair and take it to the cemetery. She was in a good mood. She likened the chrysanthemums to the *Tracht*, the costume that Johannes's mother used to wear. On the day of the commemoration of the Dead, chrysanthemums are the *Trachten* of the graveyards.

She no longer has a husband. He was playing tennis. She told him he should not have played, that he should not have been running, that he should not have gotten overheated. Why not play cards like her? So he was punished. He collapsed. It was not even too hot. There was a spring breeze, if she recalled aright. The climate is her first interest, when she gets up. Informing herself about meteorological conditions is something that her family had inculcated in her. She remembers the day of the tennis match. The spring breeze that she perceives every now and then. She thinks that it comes to visit her so that she will not forget her husband. Whyever should she forget him? She has so little to remember. She remembers that man who slept with her, in the same bed, almost without moving, so as not to disturb her. Who spent his last months in a rocking chair. After the fateful tennis match. He kept the chair motionless. His hands gripping the wickerwork armrests, his strength wholly concentrated in that gesture. In order not to rock. It was almost impossible to open his fingers. He would often turn his head from right to left, from left to right. The tennis match was still not over.

The third day at sea. Eleven days left to the end of the voyage. Among the passengers, tall and robust, the *Pfarrer*, the pastor, with his wife. He baptized me at home, in accordance with the Trinitary rite. He too takes part in the procession and is a member of the Guild. The pastor told Johannes that it had been hard for him not to stray from God. God was hostile to his person. To his vocation. He has been persuaded of this for some time. He has shown great patience in bearing divine hostility, which manifests itself at the most inopportune moments. Even aboard the *Proleterka*. In his cabin, with his little wife. Whom he had met when she was a girl. And now she is afraid of him. A churchgoer who is afraid of the pastor. She would kneel in the cabin. He would lift her off the floor, she did not weigh much. But she wanted to stay on her knees beside the bed. She did not want to sin. We are wed with the Lord's approval, said the pastor. The Lord has blessed and sanctified their marriage. The little wife could not manage to believe this. And she tried to have him share in the pleasure she got from kneeling on the floor and not being in bed with him.

I looked at Johannes. Where are his thoughts? Perhaps he had a secret place to which he could return in his mind. He is sitting beside me, in the dining room of the *Proleterka*, but he is not there. What are his empty eyes looking at? I wondered; what is it that binds him to life? I ask him to excuse me but I have to get out of the dining room. It is stifling. I head for the door, accompanied by looks of disapproval from my fellow travelers. Johannes says I can do as I wish. Outside, a grandiose solitude. I contemplate the waves. The *Proleterka* does not seem to have a destination. It sails on through the darkness and the shadows. One of the crew comes up. He is beside me. I do not turn round. I pretend I have not noticed his presence. After what seemed a long moment to me, he said something with a Slavic accent. He mentions the storm and the injured sailor. I had apparently been kind to the sailor. My gaze did not detach itself from the waves. My curiosity is strong. I do not know what his face is like. I sense his presence. On going up the gangplank, on the first day, I had noticed at least a dozen interesting men. On account of the crew, Johannes was supposed to keep an eye on me. I play for time. The water laps. I had no experience of the other part of the world, the male part. I think: you must play your cards right. We are two enemies. The sailor introduces himself. His name is Nikola P. He is the second mate. He is from Dubrovnik. His age, twenty-eight, his name and rank, proved to be more or less all I would know about him. In the space of a few minutes, I began to get a precise notion of attraction. I could not see his features clearly, but what little I could glimpse in the shadows was enough. He held the winning hand. There was no need to talk. Nor make a scrupulous examination of his looks.

I would be sixteen the following winter. In a hotel with Johannes. My birthday coincided with the week in winter that he was entitled to. When he was engaged, her family would say: "Have fun, be happy. Life smiles upon you." That way of speaking irritated Johannes. He just could not bear it. It happened when he was visiting his fiancée's family. Then Johannes went off for a walk alone, toward the lake. He walked up a path that led to his house and looked at it from outside. He looked at the garden on the other side of the wall. His twin was in the wheelchair, Jakob and Ida beside him. His parents. They were silent. It was almost dark, transparent, then opaque. Then almost nothing. The motionless shadows, the dark green of the cypresses.

The officer bids me goodnight. He goes off in a hurry. The darkness flows over the *Proleterka*. She looks like a forgotten ship. Without a crew, without a destination, only the darkness, almost tangible. The only true flag of the *Proleterka*. I go down to the cabin. Johannes is sleeping. He cannot know of the hidden passion of his daughter, the schoolgirl who wanted only the man who had appeared in the shadows without having shown his face.

At seven in the morning, *Proleterka* arrived in Crete. I think of nothing but the officer standing leaning in the shadows. Johannes has already gone up on deck. He leaves the cabin in perfect order. He has folded the sheet. The traces of sleep folded like a geometrical form. The soap is dry. A bus takes the passengers to Knossos. The light hurts Johannes's eyes. I am sitting beside him. His friend behind us. His breath. He is sleek and bronzed. He keeps on saying: "*Es ist schön*," it's beautiful, with satisfaction. I did not see the officer before going ashore. I am impatient to get back on board. As soon as you leave the *Proleterka*, she looks like a mirage. You must not look back. From the land, it looks like war surplus, circumnavigating time.

Johannes has no need of a camera, I think. Nor of memories. For him it suffices to note down the stages of the voyage. The name of the ship. *18 April: Reise nach Griechenland. Rückkehr: 2 Mai.* April 18: journey to Greece. Return: May 2. Life, in his notes, is silent and absent. Names and dates. Nothing else. Written by a man even more absent, precise in his absence. On that trip, the last he would make with his daughter, there is not so much as one word of comment devoted to Johannes. And it was also the longest period we spent together. Nor did we ever talk of that journey, afterward. On that ship that seemed to be without a rudder. As if prey to a fleeting daydream.

In front of the palace at Knossos: Johannes, gray suit, gray hat with a black band. Walking stick and dark glasses. White handkerchief in his breast pocket. White shirt collar impeccably pressed. He is exhausted. A sorrowful air amidst the passengers of the Guild. I observe him from a distance. Johannes has no summer clothes. The passengers have summer clothes. Johannes is simply sad. He is almost unaware of this. It seems as if his person embodies a stubborn Northern vocation. An extraneousness to the inclement Easter sunshine. He is motionless, I do not know where his gaze has fallen. The ladies and gentlemen of the Guild listen to the Greek woman's explanations. Stockings with a seam and a black handbag on her arm. White gloves. Johannes's friend nods at History. His camera likewise. It looks as if it is keeping time, like a metronome.

I should pay attention to the woman's explanations, says Johannes; I continue to look at her white gloves, the seams of her stockings. Her calves. "*Höre, höre zu,*" says Johannes, listen. I cannot catch the words. Only in my mind's eye can I grasp what I see. The words are too much. And the light is extremely bright. The journey is important for Johannes. The journey to Greece, father and daughter. The last and first chance to be together. But we do not know this. Or perhaps he does. Vegetation of a heartrending luxuriance. Magnificence and bane. Spring's caress sows unwitting panic. "*Höre zu,*" he says again, "*ich bitte dich,*" I pray you. He says it as if to himself. We turn our backs on the palace at Knossos. We go back to the ship. Johannes is pale. How are you? "*Danke,*" he says, he's fine thanks. He seems to be thanking his pallor. He goes down to the cabin to change. I ought to help him. But my eyes are searching for the officer. Since the previous night I had run through numerous variations of hatred toward that man who attracted me and who I did not know.

It is the fourth day at sea. Johannes and I are sitting at the usual corner table in the dining room. We are the last to go in. Johannes would like to go in earlier. I ask him to wait. I look for the officer. He is not there. My father's friend is already sitting there with his wife. And has been for years, it seems. Like the pastor and his wife. He paraded so very tall during the Guild procession. Severe and sensual. The tiny posy of flowers on the tables is delicate. They cannot find the rolling of the ship agreeable. Flowers, even cut flowers, would perhaps like to stay in a vase on dry land.

I look at Johannes. Whence comes the cold that enters his eyes? This is what I wonder, as a woman crosses the salon. Rather attractive. She was the other woman. The other female passenger aboard the *Proleterka*. I never knew who she was. She was alone. I called her "the thirty-year-old woman." Her esthetic aspect suggests that she is not a member of the Guild. She looks different. There is something unconventional about her manner. Sure of herself. She has been crossed in love and needs to get over it, I think. She heads for the captain's table. Every evening there is a guest of honor at his table. The mysterious woman sits down. She unfurls her good looks through the room. I keep an eye on her. I wanted to know her position. We are rivals. Two women on board the *Proleterka*. She pays no heed to me. She does not consider me a rival. She does not consider me at all. Yet a small blemish mars her beauty. A fleeting desperation. Her past could not interest me. The here and now, the present on board the *Proleterka*, was the only thing that counted. Her past, mine, have no importance. Two women and the crew. You don't tell the story of your own life, there's no time. Life began the moment in which we got on board. The beginning is the *Proleterka*.

From our corner table I observe. The captain's eyes, ironic flashes, are an intense light blue. He speaks many languages well. I sought complicity in his limpid, implacable gaze. I see him turn affably toward the ladies. Who had never seen anyone like him. He looks like a grand seigneur. He dispensed his favors with ill-concealed boredom. I immediately thought: he looks down on us all, that man. We who have chartered his ship. And he probably did not even like us, you know, as humankind. "The captain is *charmant*," said the Guild people. Slavs are all *charmant*, which for them means: all knaves. Pronouncing it the German way. Voicing the t. The captain had granted an audience to the provisional masters of the ship and seemed to be think-ing: "Them again." Them again at his table. Two peoples, two armies in battle formation. The people of the Guild have paid, have chartered the *Proleterka*, and they want to take full advantage of its services. There is a contract. The Yugoslavs must treat these people well for two weeks. It is possible that the crew of the ship did not want anything to do with us. Sovereignty was evident to anyone. Among the men of the crew there was a lurking sense of something eccentric, bizarre, as of those accustomed to going adrift. Sometimes, at sea, the *Proleterka* seemed as if it were steered by a ghost. By a simple and terrifying inertia.

It is twilight. Nikola on watch. Johannes in the cabin. Paler and paler. I know that I can do everything I wish. I can even take his life. Or even take my life. Ours is a family of suicides. Aspiring suicides. On the rare occasions when we have had to spend a little time, even a short spell, among relatives, the basic topic, the sole topic in which all of us showed any interest, was suicide. Unsuccessful attempts. For the rest, polite indifference. Our relatives are not interested in talking about anything else. The topic of "taking one's own life" has always been stronger than topics like money, inheritances, or illness. Not even funerals were held in any consideration. Even though they offered a pretext for meeting one another. We seldom missed a family funeral. Generally they took place in touristy spots. In pleasant spots. Where there is a lake. At the funeral dinner it was not infrequent for someone to tell of an unsuccessful suicide attempt on her own part. Many of them lived long lives.

One of us achieved his goal. It had been several years since anyone in the family had attempted suicide successfully. Our relative had gone back to live in the country. In the places of his childhood. We thought right away that the countryside had perhaps loved that little boy, but not the old man that came back. The place of his childhood turned on him. The countryside around the house was opaque. As if the infinity at the end of the fields, at the end of the path, at the end of the row of wizened trees, were mire and dust. The countryside returned the gaze of a man who would later commit suicide with discretion. His house stood in a peaceful, silent area. The peace of the places of his childhood, where he wanted to spend the last years of his life. A thought that Johannes did not have. He did not think about the last years. Since he has been alone, Johannes has almost never moved from the city with the lake, with the Guilds, with the hotel. He has never thought of going back to any place.

We wanted to know how things had gone, given the enormous and perhaps disproportionate interest that we have in suicide. None of our relatives had foregone the chance to pay him their last respects. To see his face. They said that the man had waited for twelve noon exactly, when a bell would drown out almost any other sound. He was looking at himself in the mirror. He aimed at his temple. Fired the revolver. From the window he could see the church, his hometown. The striking of the hour coincided with the revolver shot. That way no one heard.

It was summer. A sweltering summer. The sultry heat parched the trees and the peace. We go into our relative's house. They have laid him out on a table, beside the window. From the window, not a breath of wind. We gather round him. Fragile, slender, pearls at her throat, Johannes's former wife wears a bewildered look, her fingers brush the relative's hand. What was that affection she was showing for the suicide? "She is getting closer to grief." I had never seen her so moved, she was looking in the relative's face, I thought, for something that we try to see when it is too late. "Too late," I would have liked to tell her.

Since she was a believer, she wanted a priest. The priest instantly refused to hold a funeral mass in church. His superiors would not permit the coffin to enter the church for the religious service. The priest agreed to come into the house. He blesses the body. His cassock was dirty. Grease stains on his cassock. It was probably the sultriness, the terrific heat that had glued itself to his body. His face running with sweat. He could not wait to get out of that house. Like all of us, except Johannes's former wife.

The family was hot, but it was impeccable. They were prepared for the infernal climate of a sunny day in the country. Everyone was dry-eyed. Almost absent in the presence of the relative who had to be closed up as soon as possible. The flies buzzed. The sky became duller and duller. Tea and biscuits were served. We drink the tea around the relative who cannot know that the Catholic Church has rejected him. I condemn those religions that have no compassion for suicides. I condemn those who condemn. Condemn the word sinner. Words that lead to vendettas. The Church punished us too, by denying us the religious ceremony. It punished the suicide of our relative. And we all felt like suicides, unsuccessful suicides. Which has always been our vocation, for generations.

He did not even look like a suicide. The hole was tiny, his hair hid it. Everything was becoming insignificant in that house. Johannes's former wife thanks the country priest. Suddenly the refusal of a blessing in church becomes a gift. It was a gift of the Church that our relative was denied a funeral service. All that was necessary was a hasty sign of the cross, a whiff of incense, the Latin, the murmured prayers. That's enough. We thank him. We go out of our way to thank him excessively. Now the priest was feted, the guest of honor, it was he who saved us. We could not have borne other ceremonies. There is a moment, a long moment, in which everything becomes vain. Everything loses consistency. Becomes irrelevant. The priest's cassock, sanctified by then, leads the cortège. It looks as though it is floating in the shimmering haze. A handful of people walk hurriedly in the scorching heat. The vegetation pitted. Stricken. As if sprayed with acid.

They say that in the preceding days our relative had been shooting at birds. He was practicing. He had never done so before. He had several hunting jackets. He would go out for his walks wearing a hunting jacket, but he did not shoot. His dogs did not like the sound of gunshots. Of course, it's a far different thing to aim high, at the sky, than to aim in front of a mirror. At the left temple.

He had practiced by shooting a few birds. Now, some of them stop on his windowsill. There were lots of them, when they took him away.

I ask Johannes to excuse me. I have to get out of the dining room. The pastor caresses his wife's hand, as if to reassure her. The strong hand, knotty and long, and the doll's hand. I think of something carnal and violent. The pastor has never said a word to me during the voyage. His wife is sitting on the edge of her seat, her feet do not touch the floor. The pastor will give a sermon for each of the Guild passengers, when their turn comes.

A sailor brings me dinner. Nikola has arranged this. Every evening I eat on deck. I apologize to Johannes. After the *hors d'oeuvres*. In any case he always eats alone, in the hotel. Save when he is invited by his best friend. Or by someone from the Guild. They bring him his food without cutlery or glasses. He uses his Baccarat glasses and his silver cutlery. His fruit comes from a shop in the Bahnhofstrasse. Two apples. One pear. In a cardboard box. His repast is a frugal one. He swallows several pills. The table is small and round. For one person. In the hotel room, an austere order. Nothing personal, nothing to identify the room. Only the number.

Years afterward I would see the photographs of what had belonged to him. The factory too. Over one hundred years before, Johann Jakob, the founder, had established a textiles factory in a place called *Rote Trauer*, Red Sorrow. Through the town ran a river that became tinged with flame at dusk. The hour at which they tolled the bells. No believers entered the church. They were afraid to cross the bridge. Yet the bells continued to peal, to call. It was as if they were chanting the names of the inhabitants. The name of Johann Jakob. It was he who had donated the bells. Their pealing was fierce, eloquent. A runaway sermon that scourged the silence, as if out hunting for souls. As if howling out the names of Johann Jakob's descendants. Johannes's mother used to say that that place could have had no name other than Red Sorrow. That place had given them wealth. And it had taken it back. The bell ropes were pulled by a malign spirit. Johannes's twin brother's illness coincided with the loss of the family fortune. Which Johannes has always looked upon with his cold eyes. While his twin remained in the wheelchair. He struggled to look up at the sky. Even just to keep his eyelids raised. He would stare at something. As if it were the final point. He no longer noticed the changing of the seasons, as he became weaker and weaker. He lowered his head. Now he was accompanying us on the sea voyage. To see the point to which Johannes's daughter, unlike them, wishes to live. The dead twin sails, as we sail. The blades of a wind gauge idly rotate in Hades.

Johannes's daughter and the officer meet for the second time. The conversation has made no progress. The girl follows him to his cabin. It is small. A bunk, a table, two chairs. They sit down on the low bunk. The girl's clothes are on the floor, a light heap. She gives a serious smile. The officer is still in uniform. Johannes's daughter had seen the same scene in a film. What was the next sequence?

She does not want tenderness. The officer seems to foresee her desires. He bears down on her with violence. Every move with violence. Every caress. Suddenly the girl feels exhausted. Through the upper half of the porthole, dawn is beginning to break. She has the strength to get up, take her clothes, and flee. She goes back to Johannes's cabin. A brief night passes. Brief nightmares. The following day she looks tired. The day after that, she goes ashore.

On the calendar the places are the days. The visits ashore mark the time. On the program today, Santorini. The volcanic island is not shown on the participants' programs. The ship and the captain decided to put in there at the last minute. The crew unloaded us in a place that was "not included" with a certain joy. We mount the mules. Slowly. In file. The thirty-year-old woman goes before me. She waves to someone on board the *Proleterka*. I cannot see who. She is wearing colonial shorts, a silk blouse, and a big hat with a blue ribbon. Her legs elegantly draped sidesaddle across the back of the mule as if she were sitting on the edge of a precipice. And the precipice is there to admire her. Two words accompany me like a refrain: "living" and "experience." People imagine words in order to narrate the world and to substitute it. The two words must take concrete form. On the mule's back it is pleasant to mull things over. We skirt a monastery. How much time will the *Proleterka* give me for experience? She is the one in command.

Johannes has trouble in mounting the mule. I have never seen him run. I would perhaps have felt a bit uneasy, having a father who runs. He used to watch me run. He would wait for me after my skiing lessons, leaning on his stick.

He would accompany me to the ice rink, while I skated. He, who could neither ski nor skate nor run, was my motionless companion. I was consigned to him for a part of the summer and winter holidays. During the school year I was consigned to others. At six I won a ski race, the only time. At around seven I began to ski less well. Everything that he could not do, he had his daughter learn. Like tennis. And he would wait for me at the end of the match. Leaning on his stick. When my schooling was over, I stopped skiing, skating, and playing tennis.

From the heights of Santorini, I look at the landscape. The cliffs plunging down to the sea. In the distance, as if stranded, the *Proleterka*. Dozing in the spent dreams of the volcanoes. Hazy and still. In the afternoon we return on board.

A peremptory voice calls an officer. An order echoes out. The sun was taking a long time to set. One felt like pleading with the sky to get dark. The day did not want to come to an end. The captain calls again. "He's in his cabin," I say – and I add: "He is not alone." The captain pretends not to hear. In a kind and playful way he says: "Jealous." And he turns his back on me. I realize immediately that I have made an unpardonable error. I should have kept quiet. I was keeping an eye on the other one, the other woman. I had been unable to resist letting the captain know. That I knew everything that happened aboard the *Proleterka*, my ship. I informed him that the woman had not chosen him. That's all. She was in the first mate's cabin.

Professor Z.'s son is holding a glass and seems to be talking to the waves. His round, bulging eyes stare at the sea.

The fathers have not brought their children on the cruise.
Except for my father and Professor Z., who is doctor to all
the passengers on the *Proleterka*. To Johannes and me. He
vaccinated me against smallpox. His son has changed, a
pink shirt. It is open over his smooth chest with its fine,
blond down. He is wearing perfume, and smells of disinfect-
ant. He kisses my hand and sighs, sorrowfully. The trip is a
disappointment, his weary voice tells me. He concentrates
for a moment before saying why. Yes, the bunk was too
short, he could not stand it any longer. He does not want
to be a doctor. He is in the third year of medical school.
The health of the human body does not matter to him.
Nor do diseases. Every time his father cures someone he
is seized by despondency. Everyone on board is his father's
patient. The world is a perennial illness. And so, he wanted
to imply, are things of a sexual nature. "Which things?" I
ask. He is embarrassed. He bets that I too have a tiny scar
on my arm. "They think they are safe." On account of a
tiny scar. His voice is slow, nasal, monotonous.

Narbe, he keeps on repeating, scar. "You don't understand," he says. Why then is he studying medicine? Because
he has no willpower. Thanks to his lack of will, he lives.
He has given himself over completely to the enemy, to his
father. He is an only child. In him there are the unborn children of his parents' marriage. They wanted more children,
three at least. The desires of his parents have deprived him
of willpower. The unborn, in a certain sense, have deprived
him of the will to live. He had said: "No, thanks" to the
voyage. Then he found himself on the voyage. Affirmation
and negation have no sense for him. His mother, the doctor's wife, thinks she has lost two children. The unborn
drive him to study medicine. They are in agreement with

his father. Now his mother is in a clinic with bars. She wants to get out. Outside there is an extremely beautiful lawn. She sees them playing. With a tiny ball. The children must have surprisingly good eyesight, they can see what is not there. In this they resemble their mother. Their mother plays cards. They cheat. Their mother gets angry. Mother does not like losing. She goes for them. They look for the money in a black leather purse. The purse is empty. They go to rummage through their mother's bag. She pleads with them. They must not take her money. They will have it. They will have it naturally, with the will. They have no need to cheat. And in any case she has been drawing up wills for months. The children are satisfied. They take the written sheets of paper and carry them off, to the lawn. She watches at them from behind the bars. Thrilled, they read the wills in their favor.

Well, doesn't her father see? Doesn't Johannes see his daughter's behavior? It is *unverschämt*, shameless. We are in the dining room. Johannes's best friend looks with commiseration at the corner table. The neglected table. Johannes is absent and indifferent. He tries to tell me something, I should not leave the table. Immediately his voice dies away. Without conviction. Do what you like, say his clear and wounded eyes. The room sways. The waiters bring the *hors d'oeuvres*. They too no longer want anything to do with the passengers of the Guild. Politely, I get up, excuse myself. The dining room is a prison.

Nikola shoves me violently into the cabin. They must not see us. The captain can know, but he must not see us. He locks the door. He is violent on the bunk too. I had decided:

we shall do it all. I want more and more. At school, with my friend Sebastian (that's what she wanted to be called) we used to talk about sex. She wanted to do it with strangers. "Primordially," she used to say laughing. Without conversation. She is sixteen. Experienced. She would tell me things and provoke me. Now, in bed with the second mate, I think of my friend. Of her erotic and wild nature. Slim, short hair. Her nape smooth and bare. Wary. Taut as a bow. She used to say that she wanted to possess physical pleasure at all costs. There is nothing else. There was nothing else around us, she would say. She considered education harmful. We do nothing else but educate ourselves from morning till night, like a long sleep. Sebastian should have been watching us. I was behaving a little as if she were present. She was taking notes. An invisible presence in the cabin. A little smile in her eyes. "At last, you too," she would have said. Yes, at last me too.

Nikola knew how to take my thoughts too. They are in a void. He whispers a few words. I do not understand. "*Ja te ljubim,*" I love you, I say in his language in a small voice. I am exhausted. When you are exhausted you feel like continuing until you reach a kind of annihilation. Complete abandon. "That's enough now," he says in Italian. His voice comes to me like a whiplash. "Get dressed." Like an insult. "That's enough now." I throw on my clothes. There is still time. His turn on watch begins in an hour. From four to eight in the morning. He kicks me out.

"Rhodes, Delos, Mykonos": it says in the program. Three days ashore. We visit Rhodes on foot, from eight in the morning until noon. We visit everything that the program offers. The Templars' Hospital, the Templars' Way, the castle, the walls . . . It is all in the program. Johannes is fatigued. He cannot walk so much. The sun penetrates his soul, his ailing heart, his eyes, washed out and faded for generations. It penetrates his memories. In the past, burning. I think about Nikola, but I cannot avoid thinking intensely about my father. A ghost at my side. We go back on board for dinner. Shadows in the dining room. I draw the curtains alongside our little table. The light bothers Johannes. And me too. Perhaps we have the same illness. My eyes will become faded too. Our eyes are not strong like those of his wife, my mother. Like those of the women of the generations that came before her. They all had dark eyes. Even when they were blue or green.

I do nothing but look. What I do not know is where Johannes is looking. I cannot understand where he comes from. From a disused factory? From a hotel room? Yet my father and I are united by a bond, as if by a superior will, which is not of this earth. As a little girl I used to say to him: "*Sind Sie mein Vater?*" Are you my father? "*Herr Johannes, ich bin ihre Tochter,*" I am your daughter. Legally I belonged to him. I was his fourteen-days companion. His companion for a few winter days, a few summer days. And now, exceptionally, a departure from the rules, in spring. Spring is bad for him. Nature too.

Aboard the *Proleterka*, dead moments, stasis. The aftermath of the visit to the ruins. The nervous irritability that grips the passengers after visits ashore. The passengers have only just returned on board. Stunned, worn out. The visits have enfeebled their vital energies. This was spotted instantly by the crew. Who thrust them into their cabins. In captivity. Until they got their strength back. It seems as if every leg of the journey is harmful for the ladies and gentlemen of the Guild. Ruins, temples, stones, and blades of grass can be harmful. Even the *Proleterka* could be harmful for the passengers.

The third mate walks on. Robust. He walks with a rolling gait, as if it were stormy.

Johannes's daughter follows him to the cabin. He tells her to strip. He tells her to do what she does with Nikola. And no nonsense. The daughter thinks that this is part of experience. She strips and does what she does with Nikola. The mate's rough fingers fondle her. Scales. Like Nikola, he is violent. She feels as if drawn by lots. Drawn by lots by the crew. She feels pleasure in the disgust. I don't like it, I don't like it, she thinks. Yet she does it all the same. She no longer has much time. The *Proleterka* is the locus of experience. By the time the voyage is over, she must know everything. At the end of the voyage, Johannes's daughter will be able to say: never again, not ever. No experience ever again. "I want to go," she says now. The other throws her clothes at her. "Be my guest." He laughs, pointing at the door.

Entering the Bosphorus. It is the end of the journey. Three nights left. Three evenings in the dining room. Two stopovers. Istanbul and Athens. The *Proleterka* grants me a little more time to get to know Johannes. It is my last chance to know something about my father. To realize who my father is. And I avoid it. He is sitting together with some other men on the deck. Dark glasses. Dressed in dark colors. As always. I should like to go to him and tell him to stay in the most sheltered place. His friend, his best friend, is talking in a loud voice. He is laughing. Beside him, his wife, arcanum of ill luck. I look at Johannes and fear for his life. I avoid him. I can look at him from a distance. Consider his presence from a distance. I shall have other chances to know my father. I avoid knowing, as if this were the only way of knowing. I observe him. Together with the passengers of the Guild. Together with his friend. They were friends as boys, as students. Even then they went on boat trips together. On the lakes. Trips in the country. The smiling friend. Suntanned even in winter.

Johannes does not smile. The family, his family, had not yet lost its fortune. Yet he does not give even a faint smile. The expression is always the same, sad and distant. Johannes is twenty. His twin brother has not yet fallen ill. The big family home in the place called Red Sorrow looks serenely unoccupied. The factory and the chimney are a short distance away. His mother, it says in the passport, has yellow eyes. A few years after in her son's passport it would say: "Distinguishing marks: invalid."

*

The invalid, the mother with the yellow eyes, the husband the textile manufacturer: I have never met them. But I possess their documents, as well as their portraits. What there is to know, I know. The documents are closed in the drawer of a long narrow writing desk with a green leather top. I can open the drawer at any time and check. They are lying one on top of the other. The textiles manufacturer below, the mother in the middle, and the invalid twin brother on the top. I do not know how the documents came to me. They have been well kept, they look new. They are not worn like a booklet that has been handled for a long time, turned this way and that between the fingers. Inside, each one has a photograph. I do not look at the photograph of the invalid. I cannot look at it. If I look at it, I touch my own face, my own features.

The mother's eyes light up in the dark. She in her black bodice, the starched white pleats, an indefinite number of white folds, flimsy and almost transparent. Her costume, the bonnet with the lace, almost everything tends to disappear. It evaporates. But not the yellow eyes. They are a lure. The woman's heraldic device. This yellow has nothing to do with the sun. It is a Nordic yellow, the yellow after the storm. The color that is left when sky and clouds have grown calm. Leaving almost a wake, a trace of their wrath. A yellow streaked with green. The photograph has obliterated a color that comes to light again only with the word. She, closed inside the document, is called up by the name of a color.

The documents of the dead. The desk is long, it looks like a refectory table. With ink stains. Fingerprints. The three sit in their places. The woman with the yellow eyes, the textiles manufacturer, the sick son. Invalid. So the document says. They have left the family home in the place called Red Sorrow. They have also left the house in the South because it has been sold. The furniture too, auctioned off. The invalid with the wheelchair has no more barriers. He goes around the empty rooms. He persists in racing along in the wheelchair and touching the walls. With no brakes, the wheelchair is exhilarating. Nothing is left. There is still the southern sun. It filters through the garden. Someone calls. Voiceless. So, by way of a final resting place, there is nowhere else for them but my desk.

I have no ties with that family. I am a descendant with no ties. The documents prove the existence of Johannes's parents. And of the invalid. Details written in the passports, with the stamps of the journeys made. In a black folder, with a label in the center, the history of the factory. Founded in the mid-nineteenth century. In a certain sense the textiles factory belongs to me too. I have always taken a tactile pleasure in fabrics. Some fabrics repel. We have the factory documents, those three and I. I spend a lot of time in the place called Red Sorrow. I can still hear the dogs barking. What we do not possess belongs to us.

"*Du wirst diese Reise mit deinem Vater nicht vergessen.*" You will not forget this trip with your father. That is what my father's friend said at Delphi, in front of the temple. Johannes's daughter was not to forget that trip with her father. As I look at the ruins, his voice exhorts me not to forget this trip. As soon as we go ashore, his voice persecutes me. A smooth-tongued voice. At every stage of the journey, in front of every stone, Johannes's friend reminds me that I must remember. His wife's eyes glitter. Perhaps

she thinks that Johannes's daughter must remember something that she is losing. The idea that the daughter must
expiate. I walk among the ruins and try to remember. But
it is the previous night that appears. Johannes's friend
laughs. His eyes are astute slits. The vegetation is in bloom,
splendor blazing in the fields on its way to withering. To
brushwood. At Athens, in the Acropolis, Johannes's friend
comes up with his camera. "*Du wirst diese Reise mit deinem
Vater nicht vergessen.*" I was remembering the Acropolis
photographed by him.

The other night Nikola said enough. Enough. And Johannes's
daughter can still hear those words. When he, the mate,
balked. The half lover. The not altogether lover.

On the Acropolis, Johannes is exhausted. Since I must
not forget, I look at him. Indifferent, he stares at the ruins.
It is spring, and he is dressed as if it were about to snow
shortly. He is leaning on his stick. The same stick he uses
for the brief winter holidays. His pale eyes shift from one
stone to the next. What does Johannes see? I am almost
certain that, as he looks, he does not remember.

Toward the end of the trip the passengers no longer liked
one another. The expressions on their faces seemed to have
changed. A strange vertigo had seized them, an atavistic
and martial urge to crush their own companions. Even the
pastor had become agitated. He wandered around gloom-
ily, searching the sea for his sunken sermons. Everyone
suspected that at the end of the journey something terrible
might have happened.

Johannes remained aloof from those passions. Aloof
almost from himself. It was then that, for a moment, a

knowing look brought Johannes closer to the captain. A look almost of belonging to the same brotherhood. Johannes's daughter noticed that look. For the first time she felt something like joy, as if she had won a challenge. Something like pride.

Stubborn and self-righteous, the passengers are ready to leave the ship. Venice. Journey's end. On the program it says: *Auflösung*. Which also means: dissolution. At the top of the gangplank, the captain salutes them. Cold exultation in his blue eyes. Finally they are going. Slowly, Johannes goes down the gangplank. After him, his daughter. We are the last. We have no luggage. We give the impression that we have nothing. The *Proleterka* looks abandoned. It is almost as if her appearance has changed. She is more metallic, blacker. Adrift but unmoving. A sailor is scuttling around like a larva in a hurry, cursing his orders. The captain has vanished. The *Proleterka* has retaken possession of herself. And lets it show. Now it is difficult to board her. Hermetically sealed, she can only be taken by storm. She looks like a kind of mausoleum. A trophy of war. She belongs to the antiquity of the seas. Of the deeps. Of fable.

I walk slowly along the Riva degli Schiavoni. I turn round. I look for the ship. Her name is disappearing. The name *Proleterka* is corroded by the distant light, on the horizon. A few minutes dilate time. I turn round again. I wait for a wave. From an imaginary member of the crew. I wait for the officer to appear. My lover. A last wave. I would like to see his effigy carved on the prow of the *Proleterka*. We left each other without saying goodbye. Nikola disappeared the previous evening. He was not with the officers to say goodbye to the passengers. He disappeared as if he had never existed. Or only at night. As if I had not existed. And there I was, on the quay, pretending to look for something on the ground. Johannes, my father, asks why I keep on turning round. His tone is harsh. It must annoy him. I am looking for something that has no outward appearance. An amulet perhaps. How they must have irritated Johannes, those nocturnal visits to the mate's cabin. And, the following morning, the apathy of his daughter. Who was now turning round to seek the night.

The fourteen days granted to Johannes are up. My father is in a hurry. He walks as if cured of his abnormality. We pass in front of the Hotel Danieli. Johannes and his young wife had stayed there for a few days, where they were married. Johannes's wife told me that. Not he. He was unlikely to admit that he had once been married to a young woman brimming with joy and passion. He could not understand. She was impetuous, in Johannes's view. Whereas there was no impetuousness in him. So his wife lashed out. She wanted to strike, to offend, to provoke Johannes's coldness. Punish Johannes's family. And the invalid. She railed against his twin. She thought that she could detect irony in the sick man's smile. The smile that had come to him with the paralysis. And had remained with him forever. Johannes's wife could not bear that smile.

The invalid is aware that Johannes's wife detests his smile. Like non-invalids, he looked at himself in the mirror. Which stared back at him ironically. It seemed to him that his own image was mocking him. As if the mirror, as well as imitating him, wished to give a glimpse of an intention. At that point the twin brother turned the wheelchair around.

Besides, in order to know, he has no need of the mirror. He feels that on his mouth there lingers a vestige of that last expression. It was left impressed there in the final instant before the illness. Something pleasant, obscurely pleasant. What was it that had made him smile?

Unhurried, he contemplated the inexorable time that was his allotted portion. He let Johannes's wife, the silk dress, the hat, and the pearls rail against him. He continued to smile. For years. Without getting old.

I have gone back to boarding school. A few months later I go to visit Johannes. In the hotel. Where I too have a room. "How is your daughter, *das Fräulein*?" The manager of the hotel bows. He had been bowing to his client, Johannes, for many years, too many. In the hotel there also lived a family: father, mother, and son. *Die Juden*, the Jews, the manager and the concierge called them. They too, like Johannes, were permanent guests. Also for too long. Johannes and I dine in the hotel room. At the little round table. We do not have much to say to each other. The waiter sets the table, arranges the Baccarat glasses, the silver cutlery. Sometimes we dine in the hotel restaurant. At the first table as you enter, sat the manager with his wife and daughter. Three tables farther in, Johannes and I. The daughter and the manager wave and look at us, looking as we eat. Their gaze on our plates. They calculated how much they would put on the bill. Even the daughter. A little girl. We have watched her grow up. Even at five years of age she used to watch us as we ate. Barely out of the womb, she already knew how to reckon the restaurant bills of the clients of her father, the manager. She had already learned to calculate the cover charges. It cost us, or rather it cost Johannes, less to eat in our rooms. In the room, bread, cheese, and fruit were sufficient for us. While in the restaurant you had to order.

The waiter stands there and expects more orders. Some more? Anything else? The girl would look on, from her post. Her brilliantly colored eyes on our plates. She would lick the spoon that she dipped in the ice cream with hot chocolate sauce, the long and glossy pear, gluttonously. She was handsome and robust. Sometimes I wanted to go out with her. I knew no one my own age. She played hard to get. She had understood right away that I was alone. I would have had to pay for her company. It is possible that she was the one who suggested that her father, the manager, kick us out. We, the ones who paid the monthly charge.

Sometimes Johannes would take me to the Guild restaurant. The entrance is in the gallery. On the first floor, silence, the distinguished persons talk in low voices. The cutlery moves lightly almost without touching the plates. Outside, the river runs. Swans slip past. A tram goes by. Cars. When a member of the Guild dies, they hold the customary funeral dinner. Johannes feels alone. The funeral dinner for his great friend has already taken place. There in the restaurant. He did not have the time to show the photographs of the voyage. We are almost the only people in the room with the low vaulted ceiling. Johannes looks around. Perhaps he is wondering where to hold the dinner. He is wondering whether he ought to do as his friend did, to invite the members of the Guild to the Guild restaurant. Why should he think of his death? There is always Miss Gerda, in case of need. We do not talk, Johannes and I, but I manage to perceive that he wants to put everything in order, before dying. All the formalities at least. Place, restaurant, last wishes, and nothing left unfinished. I understand that he is doing this for me. All his thoughts are for his daughter.

Perhaps he is also thinking of packing up glasses, plates, and cutlery. Packing up what remains of his hotel room. We are sitting facing each other. His clear eyes continue to roam among the empty tables of the restaurant. Mentally he is filling them. He is compiling a list of names. As for the pastor, there is no need to think about that. He is the same one who was on the *Proleterka*. And he too used to look around in the ship's dining room. All would be guests of his funerary words. All guests of the Gospels that he would have read. And the invitees to the dinner? The passengers who were on the *Proleterka*.

The pastor had joined the Guild at the same time as Johannes. He had celebrated his wedding. He had baptized his daughter; later he had confirmed her. Johannes's former wife had written to the pastor asking him to send her daughter's birth certificate. The pastor sent two of them. With different dates. Perhaps he did not remember when he had baptized Johannes's daughter in the house in the city with the lake and the headquarters of the Guilds, the *Zunfthäuser*. Unless, before her, there had been another daughter about whom I know nothing. Of whom all trace has been completely lost. She bears the same name as me. She does not exist as far as the registry office is concerned. Yet the pastor had apparently baptized someone before me, born to Johannes and his wife. I have often felt the presence of another being at my side. A difficult, sick being with suicidal tendencies. A being I have never met. Who was apparently baptized a year before me. In the same house, not far from the Kunsthalle. Apparently, I have stolen its name. It stole my existence. A being that apparently tried to live in my stead. A few days after Johannes's wife received the two birth certificates, the pastor sent her a letter. He said that he had made a mistake. A mistake that I would not forget.

"*C'est le plus grand plaisir que vous ayez pu me faire, de me quitter*," said Johannes to his wife, kindly. Leaving him was the biggest favor that she could have done for him. Johannes and I are alike. He is ill. I am not yet.

Johannes and his daughter have some difficulty in accepting dinner invitations. Besides, they have few acquaintances. We know Miss Gerda's adoptive father. A strong man with a dog. A bulldog. A man that emanates vigor. He invited us to eat with them on various occasions. Johannes asked his daughter: "Do you want to go to their place?" "No." He tells Gerda's adoptive father: "My daughter has said no. Thank you." We were both wary of knowing people intimately. A dinner is always a fairly intimate situation. You go into a house where two people live together. Like Gerda and her adoptive father. The rooms and the dining room are impregnated with their presence. While we have never talked about it, we do not like going into other people's houses and eating the food that they prepare. Besides I am sure that the robust man must have done something with little Gerda. And the residue of their relationship has remained in the small apartment. Houses are not merely walls. They are often contaminated places. People should not make dinner invitations with such nonchalance. Johannes and I went to dinner almost solely to the house of his great friend. But now his friend is no more. Therefore we have no more invitations.

*

Of one thing we are certain, we have no social life. Now that Johannes's best friend has had his definitive farewell in the Guild restaurant, we have no one anymore. Save the other members of the Guild. Save the passengers on the *Proleterka*. And the murderer, who has begged Johannes several times to help him get away from the house in the South. He wants absolutely to return to the city where the mother he killed used to live. And where he served a few years in prison. This is the only precise and real detail I know on Johannes's account. He helped a murderer.

Johannes is not well. I go to visit him in the hotel. Miss Gerda urges me to stay close to my father. I leave the following day. Johannes thanks me for the visit. A few months later Miss Gerda was arranging the funeral details. In the best possible way. As soon as I arrive at the station, she sends me to the hairdresser's. She lends me a black suit. If I wish, I may keep it. She asks me if I intend to accept the will. I say yes. If I want to accept nothing. "Yes." She is the *Testamentvollstreckerin*, the executrix. She gets ten percent of all assets. I am the sole beneficiary and I can dispose of Johannes's vanished estate. Of the total lack of an estate. Miss Gerda shows me the sheet of paper on which it is written that I am the sole beneficiary. There is no salutation. There is Johannes's signature. Name and surname. Lately, when he wrote me a letter, he signed with his name and surname. Miss Gerda says to think it over before accepting. Her honest hazel eyes. Her receding chin. Every gesture impregnated with compassion and prudence. She puts me on my guard regarding any debts. And other inconveniences. Creditors. They could demand much more than I would have, she says. Than we would have. She has ten percent. Anyone could demand something from Johannes and his daughter. I could lose nothing and a bit more than nothing. So she asks me if I am sure that that I do not wish to waive Johannes's last will and testament, and she looks me straight in the eye. She passes me a sheet of paper and asks me to sign. I will not waive this nothing. I cannot waive it. Is Miss Gerda displeased? Worriedly, she gives me some coins. The boxes with the glasses, the twenty-four-piece Meissen dinner service, the silverware. Miss Gerda shows me the card announcing the bereavement. With a black border. The envelope with a black border. Heavy paper, thick. Large envelope. Well printed. Written in German. "*In tiefer Trauer*," in deep sorrow, and the name of the daughter. "*Sanft entschlafen*." Quietly in his sleep. I have no objections about the text. Miss Gerda could not have done better. It is her big moment. The man to whom she has devoted herself has gone to his eternal repose, with serenity. Without realizing it. Without suffering. At night. In the morning they called her. She wasted no time. She organized everything with the rapidity of a sparrow chirping. She chose a suit for Johannes. In crisp tones, she gave orders, paid bills, lifted the black receiver of the telephone, spoke, assuming the manner and the dignity of a widow manquée. Of a faithful woman. Of a testamentary executrix in the splendor of her duties discharged. A woman who, after having chosen a suit for Johannes, now dresses his daughter. A black suit one size too large. Severe. And who was sprucing up her hair. And her spirit. She warmly suggests that the daughter behave in accordance with the rules. Miss Gerda has invited many people to Johannes's funeral. She has invited many people to the restaurant, afterward.

*

In the chapel, the pastor, the passenger who was on the *Proleterka*, gives the sermon. He addresses the *Leidtragende*, Johannes's daughter, "she who bears the grief," and the friends. He recounts Johannes's life. He mentions when they, the pastor and Johannes, joined the Guild. They were students. The First World War had just broken out. The pastor mentions Johannes's marriage with the young Italian lady. He mentions the factory. The pastor knows every-thing about the lives of the companions of the Guild. In Johannes's name and in that of the companions he thanks Miss Gerda, the faithful assistant, for her competence . . . And again the voice of the pastor spreads through the chapel. "*Die Spuren des Alterns*," the symptoms of old age in the young Johannes, the precocious symptoms of old age in a young man. And he mentions a series of operations that the boy Johannes had had to undergo in his childhood. His daughter was unacquainted with all this. The pastor makes this known, then reads from the Gospels. In the meantime Johannes is burning. "Say thank you," says Miss Gerda. "Say thank you." I know I must say thank you. She is afraid I will not say thank you. That I may not be grateful to the words of the Gospels, to the pastor, to the fire. Outside the chapel, the black suit and that of Miss Gerda shake many hands, they offer thanks. Yet something has irked her. Johannes's daughter has refused to accept a wreath. A sumptuous wreath of flowers. Of tiny buds pinned in place. Of shrunken heads. As in certain tribes in Ecuador. No one has had pity on those corollas that a short while before were breathing in the cold wind. No, I said. Send it back. I did not want the wreath. Miss Gerda flushed. I could not, I could not send a wreath back. Johannes's daughter can not send a wreath of flowers back, she says. According to

Miss Gerda, Johannes ought to decide whether to accept the wreath or not. And Johannes has left no instructions about accepting flowers or not. Reluctantly, Miss Gerda takes a last look at the pompous wreath with the purple ribbon and the showy gilt lettering. She lets the staff take it away. It looks heavy. The manager of the hotel sent it. He sent it to his permanent guest. He can undo the wreath and make little posies for the tables in the hotel restaurant. Courtesy of Johannes's daughter. Funeral flowers and moss.

The pastor has mentioned Miss Gerda. The faithful Miss Gerda. Her name resounds through the chapel, the pastor addresses her directly. The stained-glass windows are bathed in the light of her name. Miss Gerda is moved. Not one tear. She is invisibly moved. All the passengers from the *Proleterka* are in the restaurant. It is the station restaurant. The central salon with the big lunette overlooking the Bahnhofstrasse. Miss Gerda has decided on this; this way the passengers who have come by train can leave immediately, with the lift. And the platform is right there. Almost underneath their plates. Miss Gerda is radiant. She is at the head of a long table. The ladies and gentlemen of the Guild speak to her. They laugh, they exchange pleasantries. Miss Gerda does too, seriously. She is keeping an eye on Johannes's daughter. The daughter, she thinks, is *anständig*, proper. So let it be. She is kind to each of the passengers from the *Proleterka*. She thanks. The pastor is sitting on her right. But he does not speak to her. Outside the church, besides, he is a man who talks little and observes. Whereas in the chapel his sermon had certainly not been brief. He dwelt on the precocious symptoms of illness in Johannes as a boy and an adolescent. Many operations. Much suffering.

I listened – I had not asked for the sermon – to that store-house of words. He recounted things about my father that I had never known. I felt a profound and fateful affinity with him.

Some German words left their mark, on Johannes's daughter. Said the pastor: "*Johannes bekam die Zeichen des Alterns schon früh zu spüren, schon als Kind*," Johannes had soon perceived the signs of old age, even as a child. Johannes's daughter rediscovers the German language in certain words uttered by the pastor. Like musical motifs, they accompanied her language, Italian. Some phrases said by the officer had left their mark on her in the same way. She no longer thinks about Nikola. The thought has been completely abolished. The onboard romance with the officer is over.

I heard no more of Miss Gerda. She had the ten percent. There were no creditors. Perhaps I did not thank her enough. I did not thank her for the disgust she betrayed when I tried to kiss Johannes's brow. In the ice-cold room. She was at my side. Miss Gerda thought: one does not kiss the dead. She does not know that I put a nail, a little piece of iron, in Johannes's jacket pocket. This at least I was able to do. Something that would have burned together with him. As Johannes is burning, it will keep him company. A gift from his daughter. One does not give presents to the dead. When I came out of the cold room, I knew I had left a witness to the fire.

"*Ich bin dein Vater.*" I am your father. A long time has gone by since Johannes's death and now someone is saying that he is my father. He lives in the city on the lake where for years Johannes and I had taken part in a procession. He speaks German. He has just turned ninety. He calls my mother by name. He was very much in love with her. He reels off dates. The dates might coincide. The man is glad to have found his daughter again.

I receive a letter. I read: "*Ich bin dein Vater.*" The letter ends: "*Dein Vater.*" Your father. In the middle, the story. Of when he fell in love with my mother.

On only one occasion did he see me. I was four when I went to his house, to the sender of the letter, accompanied by my mother. The woman that he loved. To offer condolences. He had a five-year-old son. Killed in an accident. The little boy had been running across the road and was run over by a car. Now he writes that I was as like his dead son as two peas in a pod. The same eyes. Even the look. It made a great impression on him, when he saw me. I was his son who had returned.

So, according to the man who says he is my father, I apparently had a brother who died at five years of age. I wonder if he is the one who has sometimes disturbed my existence.

If he is that being who perhaps wanted to live in my stead. Who was in such a hurry to meet death. I do not believe that the man is my father. I believe rather that I have a brother who had a fatal accident. And for this brother I have a profound affection. Not for the man who is talking.

I receive other letters. Sent by express mail. The handwriting clear and affected. A photograph. A face with broad cheekbones. Another image.

I do not know what impulse has led me to knock at the door of the man who says he is my father. His wife opens, wizened, extremely wizened, kind. Almost in adoration, when she sees me. The man is sitting on the veranda. The light of the garden, a sky-blue light, seems eternal. We talk on the veranda. The wife sits beside him. Her feet together. The long skirt down to her thin ankles. Flat shoes. Calm. Calm as the garden outside the veranda. A harmonious composition of elements. She must be only a little younger than he. Farther away, on a desk, photographs. Of those who have lived. Of those who have memories. Anniversaries. One Christmas bowed over another. Celebrations. I look for the dead boy. He is not there. The only person I should like to see is absent. The couple talk. Laugh. The wife knows, knew, everything, when her husband was frequenting Johannes's wife. "He was very much in love with your mother," says the wife. *Sehr verliebt*. A statement. Goodness knows why in German it sounds different, almost more real. She looks at me, sorrowful and understanding. A bitter voice without any modulation. I look at them as if I were at the theater. I have no interest in knowing. I accept my part. They are happy to have found me again. They, the house, the garden, and the furniture ooze satisfaction. A refined joy. Without excesses. Only he, the man who says he is my father, is moved. Is he sure of what he is saying? I ask him as the light of the garden fades, gently. To collect itself during the night and return the following day to the veranda where the couple are sitting. He has found his daughter again.

He invites me to stay with them. They want me to come to live in the house with the veranda, the garden, and the photographs. They insist. Even the wife insists. Calmly, she insists. The same tone. They show me the room. They show me all the rooms. I move as if I were in my own home. By this time I have worked into the part. Johannes's daughter playing the part of another man's daughter. They beg me to come to live with them. They say that I must have had a hard life. No, I say. Very easy. They look disappointed. The air of commiseration remains in place. They are convinced that I have had a hard existence. She in particular. They talk. He is a scientist. He has held many conferences. You can see that he is accustomed to public speaking. To speaking to a daughter who has been found again. I let them speak. Sitting close to each other. Long-lived and wealthy.

He had thought that he would say nothing. He had set his mind on saying nothing. Again in agreement with his wife. Benignly in agreement with his wife, with the rooms, the photographs, the objects, his worktable, his conferences, the windows. All converged in the decision to say nothing. Once he turned ninety, he could bear it no longer. He had to speak out. "Why?" I ask. It is curiosity that prompts me to talk. I am sitting facing him. He: *"Wahrheitsliebe,"* for love of the truth. He had to speak for love of the truth. The only chance he had. His wife nods. She repeats: *"Wahrheitsliebe"*

84

in a harder tone. She seems ruled more than he is by love of the truth. She nods doggedly, evangelically, starkly. The truth has no ornaments. Like a washed corpse, I think. She has understood that, had they not found her husband's daughter, the life remaining to them would have been a torment. He talks of nothing but his daughter. He does not want to die before seeing his daughter. It is his only desire. And so they found her again.

It all coincides. But it is not proof. I did not want proof. I listened to them. I listen as the scientist talks of my mother. I am glad that someone is talking of her. Who has never said a word. My mother never had any need to make confessions. Neither to me, nor to my father Johannes, nor to others. Not even on her deathbed did she wish to talk. I was at her side. She could have done so. She said nothing. Peremptory. In her sleep and in her last hours. Without strength. Merely with the will to say nothing. I was not to know. But the scientist at the age of ninety had not managed to say nothing. In that moment I had a great liking for my mother. Who abandoned us, Johannes and me. But she did not talk. I have her Steinway. Her jewels. The memory of a woman who did not feel the impulse to tell her daughter whose daughter she really was. She asks for extreme unction furtively. To the nurses: "Don't tell my daughter." She did not want to give the impression that she was about to die. She removes my hand with delicacy. I must not touch her. I watched. She is no more. Outside the window, a palm tree.

Now this man is telling me about my mother. He is telling me all that she preferred not to say. My mother did not have a love of the truth, *Wahrheitsliebe*. In German it is a compound word. The pastor, in his farewell sermon, had also used a few compound words. For example: *Leidtragende*, "she who bears the grief." This is how he addressed Johannes's daughter. And the "esteemed participants in mourning," those from the *Proleterka*.

I wonder if it were not sufficient for the alleged father to know, and to have seen and met me when I was a girl. At ninety it is not enough. The truth is gluttonous. He wants more. He wants his daughter close by. He wants to talk to her. Look at her. Kill her, I think. The homicidal instinct of this rich, healthy man, who knows how to speak. And who uses many compound words. The homicidal paternal instinct. The instinct of mine and yours. Of possession. *Dein Vater. Meine Tochter*. Your father. My daughter. A futile round of possessions.

"You have to know." It is she who is speaking. Her half-shut eyes in the long, waxen face are staring at me. Her voice inflexible. Her tone is placid, submissive. With the timbre of one who is superior. "You were not the one," I should like to tell her, "who made my mother pregnant." She is so sure of herself, that woman. Sure that it was she who, by divine intercession, caused my birth through her husband. Her hands clasped, her body composed, her head bowed, she looks at the ground. And is silent. The house is silent.

I went to the cemetery. I looked in vain for Johannes's name. The concession had expired. It seemed to me that Johannes said thank you for having remembered him, but not to look for him any more.

My brother had been in a hurry to die. He ran to meet death. While I was closed up in a room. We lived not far from each other. The same district. But I know this only now. The man who says he is my father has no need to insist that the dead boy is my brother. I have always known I have a brother. I have never been alone. I think that we were very close: he in death, I in life. It does not matter to me if the man who says he is my father really is my father. All that matters to me is to know that I have a brother. I cannot explain the immensity of the love I have for that boy who ran. The love that one has for simulacra. For that which is not visible, but has light. For a little boy with a passionate wish to die.

"You were more or less the same age: he was one year older." Today that little boy would be over fifty. This seems to frighten them. That the boy, were he alive, would be over fifty. From their reaction, it seems that they would never have wished something of the kind. As if the boy were predestined to die at that age. It had to be a premature death. And that is all. You do not think of the age. You get used to it. A child died. Calculating the age he would be today makes them tremble. They have always thought of him as a little boy. And the subsided grief regarded a boy, that physiognomy. On the day in which I went to make the visit of condolence, for a moment they mistook me for him. I am almost the same age. "But with you it is different." I cannot understand why every so often they speak in unison.

"You were more or less the same age." The wife repeats that we were *sehr ähnlich*, very alike. Now, finally, I know who would have lived in my stead. Perhaps my brother could not bear my being alive, in an overcoat like his, an exact copy of himself. After that visit of condolences, the one who says he is my father never looked for me. He had other children with his lawful wife. "Now they are ill," he says. It seems as if he could not care less about the remaining children. Nor do I care about the other children, about the other two. The alleged father continues talking, his children are my half brothers, he says, but he is interrupted by the patient voice of his wife: "One is dead." The presumed father makes a vaguely irritated gesture. "*Natürlich weiss ich*," of course he knows that. As if to say: "*Es ist schon gut*," fine. Fine for me too. One is left. The survivor. I am not curious to meet him. I think only about my brother. Of his impatience to die. It is with him that I have a bond. Since I went to his house on a visit of condolence. With my mother, at that time still Johannes's wife. What would she have said to him? I am going for a walk, I am going to a friend's, or with a serious and hasty air: I have to go to a funeral. It is already late. On the day of mourning she took me to her lover's house. To let him see his daughter, while the other one, the brother, had just died. To let him see his daughter, the resemblance with the little boy. While he was exposed to people's gaze. When my mother and I went into the house everyone's eyes were upon us, on the striking resemblance between the two children. The boy laid out and the girl standing looking at him. "They look like brother and sister," someone said.

The tone of my voice changes. I realize that I am speaking German. As if that language had been imposed on me. The language of funerals, of sermons, of the Guilds. I have prepared a tiny glossary of the German words that have marked a destiny. That have changed the course of a life. A caprice of fate has permitted the repetition of the word love, love of the truth, to the point that the word and its meaning are annulled. By my alleged father, before he was swept off the face of this earth.

I ought to understand. I ought to understand the truth. The malevolent and idolatrous passion for the truth that has stricken the couple like a disease. The alleged father and his austere, fervid spouse. To tell the truth when it no longer makes any sense. When it is useless. The stubborn frivolity of the old. These two are a smug pair. Telling the truth and hurting. They say that they were obliged to tell me it. She is sorry if they have hurt me. I must understand. As long as they do not utter the word truth again.

A farewell is obligatory. The man who says he is my father has understood that he must hold his peace. The silence of shadow. In his eyes a sweet and desolate expression. Toward the woman he calls his daughter. Toward things doomed to disappear.

"Why now?" They had had all the time in the world. He, the scientist, has a ready reply: because now we are becoming *vergesslich*, forgetful. They are losing their memory. That is why they had to speak now. Not tomorrow. They have revealed their secret out of precaution. Thanks to this precaution I have met the man who says he is my father.

He had left sheets of paper in all the rooms. Hundreds of sheets. Upon them it was written that I was his daughter. He wanted to let it be known at all costs. If anyone had torn up one sheet, another would have remained. And another again. As if sheets of paper were suddenly sprouting from the floor, like little ghosts.

Now he has talked for love of the truth. Gradually he forgets everything. Even his daughter.

Dear readers,

As well as relying on bookshop sales, And Other Stories relies on subscriptions from people like you for many of our books, whose stories other publishers often consider too risky to take on.

Our subscribers don't just make the books physically happen. They also help us approach booksellers, because we can demonstrate that our books already have readers and fans. And they give us the security to publish in line with our values, which are collaborative, imaginative and 'shamelessly literary'.

All of our subscribers:

- receive a first-edition copy of each of the books they subscribe to
- are thanked by name at the end of our subscriber-supported books
- receive little extras from us by way of thank you, for example: postcards created by our authors

BECOME A SUBSCRIBER,
OR GIVE A SUBSCRIPTION TO A FRIEND

Visit andotherstories.org/subscriptions to help make our books happen. You can subscribe to books we're in the process of making. To purchase books we have already published, we urge you to support your local or favourite bookshop and order directly from them – the often unsung heroes of publishing.

OTHER WAYS TO GET INVOLVED

If you'd like to know about upcoming events and reading groups (our foreign-language reading groups help us choose books to publish, for example) you can:

- join our mailing list at: andotherstories.org
- follow us on Twitter: @andothertweets
- join us on Facebook: facebook.com/AndOtherStoriesBooks
- admire our books on Instagram: @andotherpics
- follow our blog: andotherstories.org/ampersand

Current & Upcoming Books

Translated into about twenty languages, FLEUR JAEGGY is a true original of European writing. The *Times Literary Supplement* named Jaeggy's *Proleterka* as a Best Book of the Year, and her *Sweet Days of Discipline* won the Premio Bagutta as well as the Premio Speciale Rapallo.

ALASTAIR MCEWEN was born in Dunfermline, Scotland, in July 1950. To date, he has published over sixty book-length translations (novels and non-fiction), essays, articles and poems, plus several feature-film scripts and operatic librettos. He has worked with some of Italy's finest living writers: Baricco, Busi, Eco, Jaeggy, Tabucchi and Veronesi.